Furry Paw, Middle Claw

A novel

by Barry Jackson

Turn the Page
PUBLISHING

Published by Turn the Page Publishing LLC
P. O. Box 3179
Upper Montclair, NJ 07043
www.turnthepagepublishing.com

Although the story was inspired by true events, this is a work of fiction.
Characters are fictional, a composite drawn from several individuals and from imagination.
Though certain locations are real, the events, dialogue and scenes that figure
in the narrative are products of the author's imagination and are used factitiously.

ISBN-13: 978-1-938501-10-4

ISBN ebook-13: 978-1-938501-11-1

Furry Paw, Middle Claw
Library of Congress Control Number 2012950504

PRINTED IN THE UNITED STATES OF AMERICA

Edited by Dorothy Jackson
Cover Artwork—Original Painting by Cynthia Swink Medlin
Cover Design by Robin McGeever, McB Design

DEDICATION

To my wife Dorothy, my son Ian and all the cats who have been in our lives: Robin, D'Artagnan, Sammy, Timmy, Dash, Oscar, Scallion, Fly, Peter, Lucky, Glacier and Luna.

ACKNOWLEDGEMENTS

To my wife, Dorothy, who introduced me to cats, and through them, opened my heart to write this book. With her constant support and superior editing, the story came to life with a rich and heartfelt voice.

Thanks also to my publisher, Roseann Lentin, for her invaluable inspiration and editing. And to everyone in my life who, for better or for worse, shaped my experiences to make me the man I am today.

TABLE OF CONTENTS

INTRODUCTION

By nature, I'm not an animal person. Growing up, dogs bit me and cats, well, were cats. When my wife, Dorothy, first introduced her furry felines into my life, I didn't relish the invasion of my personal space and fur slathered on everything I owned. At the time, I didn't understand the seemingly one-sided investment of time and money that people devote to their pets. Therein, lies the story.

Barry Jackson

CHAPTER 1
TESTAMENT

I was born and raised in a working man's town where the men who toiled in the Newport News Shipyard and the women who raised their children and tended their homes were veterans of hard times. Long before they were born, their fathers had returned from the horrors of trench warfare in the fields of France and Germany. As the precarious building blocks of the Great Depression toppled into disaster, many grew up in hunger and want. Just when there appeared to be light at the end of a very long tunnel, America was, once again, at war. And these young men, not old enough to vote or buy a beer, were on their way to war in Europe or the South Pacific.

Once again, families kept an anxious vigil where every telegram or knock on the front door could mean the death of a beloved. After the war, sons joined their fathers at the shipyard; some queued behind them at security checkpoints, others shared a laugh during lunch and those, who were laid to rest so far from home, walked beside their fathers as incorporeal shadows of unspeakable loss.

In the post-war years, sonic booms from Langley became as common as the call of the cardinal and wren as children gazed up from their play to watch in wonder as their futures were writ in the vapor trails that crisscrossed the sky. Yet, it remained a place where dogs could snooze without fear in the middle of a country road on a summer's afternoon and stores were closed on Sundays. The townspeople learned to straddle two eras as they commuted to jobs in aerospace while carefully preserving the colonial traditions of a bygone age, when the idea of America was green and democracy was still considered an experiment.

My father was in Texas training as a pilot when World War II ended. Soon after he returned home, he met my mother and was smitten by her beauty as well as her faith. His sandy brown hair, well-scrubbed looks and infectious humor immediately endeared him to my mother and within a year they fell in love and quietly married in a little church near Williamsburg. My parents rented a house not far from the shipyards, and Mom, who had just graduated high school, began her first job as a bank teller. Dad became an apprentice shipbuilder and hitched a ride with his older brother until he could save up enough money to buy his own car. Every work day, they joined the multitude of men who drove through the yard's imposing security gate at Washington Avenue, manned by armed guards who brooked no argument and effectively kept the rest of the sleepy little southern town and all curiosity seekers at bay. Past another checkpoint, where Dad would eventually display his Top Secret security clearance, he joined young and old alike as he made the steep descent down steel and concrete steps to the shipyard proper where most of the men faced a long, rarely enjoyable, trek to their job site.

When the wind blew in from the south, the air was suddenly sweetened with the fulsome aroma of raw tobacco being loaded in cars at the rail yard down river, briefly displacing the harsh fumes of diesel and welded steel. In winter, bitter winds off the James lashed rain and snow upon thousands who, with each step, yearned for fairer skies and warmer days. However, when summer came, the sun would prove to be no friend. Its rays bore down, relentless and unimpeded, conjuring up elusive, shimmering pools that promised relief but delivered none. It wasn't an easy place to work. The noise level in the dry docks and millhouses could exceed 100 decibels while the unyielding concrete took its toll on the backs and joints of the men. Dad said he could always tell if an old man had worked at the yard; he would be stone deaf by sixty with bum knees, hands riddled with arthritis, and all the hair on the inside of his legs would have been walked off years ago. Still, the young flocked to the shipyard despite the evident ravages of the old. A love of the sea and the ships that sailed upon her ran deep here.

Two years after my parents married, my brother was born, healthy and strong. They bought a home in Hampton and Mom quit her job to dote on her first born, spending any free time singing with the church choir and frequently playing hostess to her large family of ten brothers and sisters, their spouses and children. Being alone was unnatural to my mother; she loved visitors, so my parents' door was always open with a restaurant-sized coffee maker at the ready to warm and welcome family and friends. The next eight years were happy ones as my brother thrived in school and Dad was now a foreman.

Just before their tenth anniversary, my mother's fondest wish was granted. She was expecting again and it was no secret to family and friends that she wanted a girl. In a heartbeat, my birth laid waste to all the years of fervent prayer and defying doctor's orders; her dream of a little girl was over. When the doctor slapped my bottom and cried, "It's a boy," my mother's smile froze like her heart, making her immune to the congratulations that besieged her, as she began to nurture a deep, inconsolable disappointment. My father wasn't too happy, either. Dad never wanted another child, male or female; he was satisfied with his family of three.

My brother and I could not have been more different. He was an "easy" baby and I seemed to challenge my mother at every milestone. I was colicky as an infant and nearly died of colitis before my first birthday. Like most toddlers, "no" became my favorite word, and I vigorously rebelled against any impediment to my personal freedoms. When my mother wasn't looking, I would run out of stores and, on more than one occasion, I escaped from the babysitters during church services. My *piece de resistance* was the time I locked my fastidious mother out of the house, took every pot out of the cupboard and sprinkled an entire box of Tide all over the kitchen floor. My poor mother; first, I tried her soul, then her patience. Soon, "Dean stories" became the stuff of family legend.

One Saturday morning, I was awakened by the unmistakable bubbling of the percolator brewing thick, strong aromatic coffee. Various aunts and uncles chatted happily at the crowded kitchen table as I padded down the hall to our bright yellow kitchen with the big fork and spoon on the wall and Mom's new refrigerator in a funny shade of green. I stood by the kitchen doorway, small and undetected, wanting breakfast before watching my favorite cartoon, *Crusader Rabbit* when I heard Mom mention my name. Anxious to hear what she had to say and sure that she would brag about the "A"

I got in my spelling quiz, I ducked behind the door. While waiting for my moment of glory so I could pop up and surprise them, I was the one who was surprised. Instead of praising me, my mother said she was sorry I wasn't a girl. A frisson of shock sent me sliding to the floor. My heartbeat drowned out the rest of the conversation until I realized I'd be in big trouble if they found me listening. When Uncle Frank rose to get more coffee, I ran to my room, unseen once more, to try and make sense of what seemed incomprehensible - my mommy never wanted me.

I carefully closed my bedroom door, grateful I wasn't seen. I stood silently among all the other inanimate objects, unable to wrap my seven-year-old brain around what I had just heard. My mother said she didn't want me. Mom even said she prayed to God for a girl. Questions no child should ever ponder burst forth in a merry–go–round of panic and confusion. Why was God mad at her? Was I to be her punishment? Was I bad? Shame overwhelmed me as I realized that I was responsible for making my mother sad, and I didn't know how to make her feel better. I jumped when my brother banged on my door, telling me to get dressed. I took off my pajamas and stood in front of my mirror naked, pale and scrawny as goose bumps blossomed all over me in the chill of an October morning. Unsure what to make of me or my place in the world, I dressed and just as I finished buttoning my favorite plaid shirt, Mom poked her head in my room. Smiling, she told me *Crusader Rabbit* was on. I ran to her and burst into tears, wrapping my arms tight around her legs, rubbing my runny nose on her freshly ironed dress. I wanted to tell her I was sorry, I would be a good boy, but the words stuck in my throat. When she put her arms around me, a small note of rebellion sparked in my heart as I wondered what was real: the person hugging me or the one who said she had always wanted someone else.

At seven, I had no idea I was at odds with a phantom in a race I could never win. Mom continued to persevere at every holiday and family get together, foisting her disappointment on anyone who would listen. As if it made any difference, she capped off each performance with a brave smile, as she offered the kind assurance,

4

"… but I fell in love with him when I saw him." That proviso never erased my fear that somewhere behind her eyes lurked the cherished image of my girly *doppelganger* that would haunt me for years. In time, I became adept at dodging this soul crushing nonsense. I slept late or I laid low in my room until the sorry spectacle of Mom nailing herself to another cross was over. Eventually, I made peace with the notion that my birth was just like being given a brand new Mercedes *but* with a large scratch on the driver's side door. It's still nice, but…

CHAPTER 2
THE PROMISED LAND

Soon after what I have always referred to as my "personal dawn of consciousness," a grey kitten with blue eyes pawed at the back door. I could barely hear its cries over the raucous laughter in the dining room. My hands gently lifted and cocooned his ragged, wet body as I begged my mother to let me keep it. There is no question that my parents' reaction was tempered by the presence of guests in the house; otherwise, at best, the kitten would have been relegated to the dubious fate of a shipyard mouser. Still, Mom adamantly refused to have a dirty animal in the house so the kitten was consigned to the garage where it ate table scraps and learned not to trust, staying quiet and shy. I was forbidden to even give the kitten a name.

Miraculously, the kitten thrived on the meager succor doled out to him, and six months later, one sunny spring day, he wandered off, never to return. Before he left us, I noticed a pronounced middle claw that he flashed whenever my parents were near. I didn't know what it meant at the time but I would *learn* later. For a long time, I included this grey kitten in my prayers and hoped he found his way to a better life and a loving family. Somewhere deep in my soul, I tucked away this lesson in survival and learned to be patient, biding my time till I was also strong enough to leave.

Two months later, strikes crippled the shipyards and I was thrown one of life's rare opportunities. While Dad walked the picket lines, Mom returned to work. Since I was too young to stay by myself, she arranged for our next door neighbors, the Meyers, to take care of me until she got home. Hallelujah, I was delivered from boredom. No more hiding in my room trying to think up clever retorts to my older brother's taunts, or dreading when Dad would come home from work and deliver his daily dose of censure and scolding from behind his newspaper.

Not that staying with the Meyers would be a picnic. Mrs. Meyers was my crazy piano teacher and her son, Mark, was my best friend. Mark was two years older than me and a brilliant pianist who uttered the vilest curses every time he hit the wrong note but I loved listening to him play, especially when he would insert a rock 'n roll riff into Beethoven or Liszt.

Every Tuesday I had a piano lesson promptly at 4:00 pm. I would sit at their baby grand piano in the pink parlor with the frilly curtains and enormous silver tea service waiting for Mrs. Meyers' grand entrance. Mrs. Meyers' perfume would always precede her. Mark said it was called "Youth Dew" but it smelled more like *youth poo.* It was hard not to gag as she opened the double doors with a flourish and wordlessly glided into the room with Maggie, her Dachshund, at her heels. Every lesson was the same, Mrs. Meyers looked like she was about to go to a party. She always wore a fancy dress and had two heavy strands of pearls around her neck. Her hair was piled high on her head and her long nails were always polished. The room was dead silent until she finished smoothing her dress, her bracelets tinkling as she patted the space between us so that Maggie, also reeking of *youth poo,* could jump up, leaving me only one buttock's worth of space on the piano bench. Only then would the silence be broken, when she turned to face me, smiling, and asked my now eight-year-old self the dreaded weekly question.

"Child, how many people have you brought to Christ this week?"

The Meyers were rich in comparison to other families in the neighborhood who lived in newly-built small, three-bedroom brick houses. They had the most spectacular Christmas light display in town, and every summer the family held a Fourth of July picnic to ply the community with their largesse and rustle up more business for Mrs. Meyers' studio. The Meyers' home imbued a faded, if downright rickety, southern gentility. The three-story white washed farmhouse had black shutters, some missing a slat or two, while others hung from a single hinge due to last year's blizzard. Its roof had three chimneys, all lopsided and infested with squirrels. The middle one, in particular, was in serious danger of collapse due to a Great Blue Heron that loved to make her nest there and no amount of noise would dissuade her. The driveway, hopelessly riddled with axle-busting potholes, meandered from the main road for about half a mile through a haphazard concoction of foliage. Tall and elegant Magnolias grabbed the lion's share of the sunlight as the pink and red Crepe Myrtles vied for the remaining dappled rays with the honeysuckle that insinuated itself round their gnarled limbs.

Mr. Meyers spent all his time in the fields. The only time I ever saw him was at the kennels where they kept English Pointers. Their house was always full of dogs because, unlike more unscrupulous breeders, they never abandoned or destroyed a less than perfect pup. Unfortunately, the Meyers were also suckers for strays so when a six-month-old mongrel, with ragged ears and a belly full of worms, appeared in their yard, the pup, without question, was welcomed into their family. This was so different from my parents' reaction to the grey kitten and, ultimately, *me.*

Every day after our homework was finished, and sometimes even if it wasn't, Mark and I gobbled our snack and ran out to play. When Mrs. Meyers was giving piano lessons, we were banned from the house anyway and that was just fine with us. We played catch, rode our bikes up and down deserted country lanes, and worked on our fort near the creek that bordered their property. When we got bored with these mundane pastimes, we invented a game involving tree branches and the electrified fence that Mr. Meyers installed last year to keep his cows from wandering into a neighbor's melon fields. To prove our burgeoning manhood, each of us would hold a branch against the electrified fence to see who could hold it there the longest. The surge was undeniable but not incapacitating. Fear would always rush up from my stomach to tell my brain this was really stupid but I had something to prove; to me and anyone else watching. If Mark felt any trepidation, he never showed it.

Though Mark and I both chafed under at the suffocating edicts of our Bible Belt mommas, we handled our frustration in very different ways. Mark was as rebellious as I was reticent, and I always admired him for his gumption. Mark saw his mother's sanctimonious behavior as a mean-spirited attempt to belittle and control everyone around her. Coming from my hamstrung household, it was exhilarating to see my friend fearlessly wage a guerrilla war and even get away with it sometimes. The surprise was that Mr. Meyers rarely got in the middle of it; maybe he had given up trying and decided to let his son take a crack at his wife. In fact, the only time I ever saw Mr. Meyers punish Mark was the day he painted the minister's cat blue, and, even though he spent the entire summer copying the Bible, I believe Mark considered that his finest hour.

The strike at the shipyard was almost over and my parents' mood was improving every day. As a reward for getting straight A's on my spring report card, Mom let me invite Mark for a sleepover. I was so excited that a friend was coming over and Mom had promised to make waffles for breakfast. After dinner, Dad took my older brother to baseball practice and Mom called to say she had to work late, so we left our dinner dishes in the sink and raided the kitchen. Armed with candy, soda and chips, we fashioned a nest of sleeping bags, pillows, and an old comforter and hunkered down in front of the television set to watch horror movies on *Shock Theatre*. It was barely 7:30 when I heard Mom open the back door. Mark and I yelled "hello" and continued our debate about whether or not vampires lived in the church cemetery down the block.

"Dean!" shrieked Mom, "Why are these dirty dishes still in the sink? Why hasn't the garbage been taken out? I've been working all day and this house is a pigsty."

She slammed down her purse and stormed into the living room.

"Get in here and clean this kitchen, now. I am not going to put with this, company or no company."

Mark stared as if he had seen a train wreck and was rendered speechless, something new for a smart aleck who had an answer for everything. I sprang to my feet, quaking with fear as I hurried to the kitchen, cringing as I passed her, fully expecting to be struck. I knew it was pointless to argue or make excuses. Mom was hard on my heals shouting her familiar invective of how Robert would never have been so disrespectful, he understood what it was to be member of this family, and everyone had to pull their own weight. By the time I reached the sink, I was crying so hard I could barely see as I reached for the sponge and dish soap. She stood over me continuing her rant as I washed the two plates and two forks with spaghetti sauce on them. I cried so hard that I couldn't catch my breath and was ordered into my room to calm down. I ran to my room and slammed the door.

"Do you see?" shouted Mom to Mark. "Do you? What I have to put up with!"

I sat on my bed, chest heaving as I strained to hear Mom telling Mark how I never did anything around the house. I was lazy. She never had any help and I was more trouble than I was worth. Like that morning a year ago when I heard her say to all the people in my world that I was not wanted, I had to fight down the shame that rose up to crush me. All my supposed faults, like gaping wounds, had been laid bare for my best friend to see. I started to cry again when she pounded on my door and told me I was keeping my guest waiting.

After Mom slammed her bedroom door and switched on her TV, I hoped it was safe to return to the living room. Mark reached out his hand and helped me sit beside him. I couldn't meet his eyes; all I wanted was to disappear inside the old comforter and not come out ever again. Mark gave me a soda and asked if I was alright. I was so thirsty I drank it all in one gulp and promptly threw up my humiliation, the spaghetti, and the Pepsi. Mark, who had a lot of experience in covering his tracks, helped me clean up my mess. Since Mom's closets reeked of moth balls, we grabbed some and rubbed them over the stain on the comforter to hide the smell.

"Wow, I am so glad I don't have your Mother!" said Mark.

Even though I had just been flayed raw by my mother's tirade, I was shocked by Mark's opinion of my mother, especially since his only aim in life was to rail against his testy, self-righteous mother. I shrugged my shoulders in grudging acknowledgement but struggled with the urge to defend her. It was a strange experience to be wounded and vindicated all in the same breath.

CHAPTER 3
THE BARN

Things would change. Mark and I began to grow apart. Maybe it was the aftermath of the sleepover or the forced fellowship five days a week. Though we still spent time together every afternoon playing catch or Clue, something was lost and I felt the growing chill of isolation once more. At the instigation of the preacher whose cat had been painted blue, Mark was to spend the entire summer at a Bible camp somewhere in North Carolina. The day after Mark left, I overheard Mrs. Meyers telling my mother that as the bus pulled away Mark made an obscene gesture to the preacher. The reverend became apoplectic and chased the bus for eight blocks before he gave up. Involuntarily, I let out a whoop of happiness and ran to my room to stuff a pillow over my head to muffle my laughter.

Since all my other friends lived far away, I really missed Mark. I started the summer with Mrs. Meyers and got frequent updates on Mark's rocky road to becoming a better Christian. She gave me free piano lessons whenever she had the time and I even made friends with Maggie the "Weiner" dog, taking her for long walks. Even though I was alone most of the time, anything was a welcome change from what waited for me at home every night. Mom and Dad had started to fight again. I don't know about what because every time they started, I just went to my room and closed the door. Turning on the radio or my record player, I did my best to drown out their harsh words. As always, Robert had an easy out; he would just call his best friend, Roy, whose father had bought in a brand new Corvette Stingray for his birthday, and they would disappear for a couple of hours until things cooled down. Eventually, I fled the house too and found a warm retreat in the Meyers' rickety old barn. My heart whispered there were lessons to be learned there.

Long ago the barn must have been a brilliant red, bright enough to be seen from far away. Now the faded paint peeled and flaked in brittle strips, scattered by the merest breeze, revealing weathered two by fours, black with rot and scarred by termites. The wind whistled a melancholy and staccato tune through the tin roof pockmarked by decay. When it rained the droplets sounded like popcorn popping with the manure and sweet hay replacing the aroma of melted butter. A broken-down thresher sat idle and rusting in a far corner as field mice skittered in and out of empty feed bags hoping to discover a tasty morsel.

I was ill at ease when I was alone with the horses, but somehow I managed to summon the courage to approach a stall, trying hard not to startle at the first stray whinny. Alert for any sign of unwelcome, I would cautiously extend my hand to offer a pat on the head or scratch behind the ear. Slowly, I grew a bit more comfortable in their presence and I think they considered me favorably too. I knew I needed to be here in the barn to bear witness to the care these lives received, not because of what they could earn or produce, but because they belonged to the Meyers family and that would always be enough.

Now that it was warm, the horses spent most of their time in the pasture but the barn still bustled with life. Rock doves cooed high overhead and the barn owls, that maintained a residence in the topmost corner of the roof would fly off every evening at dusk for a night's hunting. In time I learned to relax around the animals, even Samson, their hulking black stallion. It was a peaceful place, and I was happy there, but the colony of feral cats that lived near the barn gave me the willies. I never knew where they were or how many there were in the barn at any given time. Even in daylight, their eyes glowed red in the dark recesses of the barn. From the hay loft to the tack room, I heard their disembodied trills and unearthly yowls as they stealthily explored the empty stalls or dug through the hay in the loft. Worst of all were the grisly remains of mice, voles, birds, even the occasional rabbit littering the barn floor. This all served to daily temper my solitude with unsettling reminders that I shared my sanctuary with a multitude of hunters whose instincts had been indelibly formed millennia ago and could not be tamed. I wasn't to be moved, however. Most days I would bring a radio, book, pens, and paper and settle in to read, draw, sing along with Elvis or just be in my private sanctuary without fear of ridicule or intrusion.

I knew it was getting late one afternoon when I heard the familiar whistle from my father signaling it was time for dinner. I slammed my book shut, hating that he called for me like a dog and never did it to Robert. I stomped over to the hay loft door, angrily crunching the bales of hay with each step. I saw my father round the paddock with Robert in tow. My brother was busy kicking up dirt, making it clear that he was bored and would rather be anywhere else. I leaned out of the loft and waved to them. Dad gruffly nodded in response.

"Come on, boy," he said, his voice silky with promise, as he strode forward and stood below me with his muscular arms raised. I eyed him and the ten foot drop to the ground and thought he was crazy; the back ladder was safer.

"No, Dad," I said and headed for the back ladder. "I want to climb down."

"Chicken," mumbled Robert.

My father was so tall that with his arms raised it was only about a two foot jump, yet my stomach knotted just like when I held the branch on the electric fence. Moments of hesitation seemed like hours. The longer I kept him waiting, the louder my father's voice rose, repeating the same command over and over, "Jump." Finally, Dad's smile flattened and faded away. He was embarrassed, but it was more than that—he was in a hurry, like he was telling a joke and anxious to get to the punch line. I stood before him, twisting clumps of straw in my fists, sick with guilt, but I still did not jump until Dad played his favorite trump card that was sure to breach any impasse.

"Your mother is waiting," said Dad, now sure of my compliance.

I cautiously edged to the threshold, glancing at Robert for reassurance, but his eyes remained firmly fixed on the bottle cap he was flipping over with the toe of his sneaker. His cheeks were red and his voice silent.

"Now," said Dad.

I obeyed, and in the blur of gravity, I saw my father withdraw his arms and step away.

I tried to break my fall but I hit the ground hard. The breath shot from my chest like a pistol as I lay sprawled face down, my hands deeply imbedded with pebbles, dirt and hay. A dull pain gripped my stomach as I fought to catch my breath. I wanted to vomit. I tried to focus as tears burned my eyes, waiting in vain for a helping hand or contrite word. Only the cats, usually silent and invisible, angrily voiced their indignation on my behalf. Bits of hay displaced by my landing now rose lazily forming a golden aura around me in the late afternoon sun, choking my nose and mouth with dust and pollen. When I sneezed, I could have sworn that my head exploded.

"Geszundheit," my father said, chuckling at his dry wit, refusing to assist me as I tried to stand. Shaking, I managed to get to my knees and noticed that my pants were bloody and torn.

"That should teach you never to trust anyone," said Dad, and the three of us walked home as if nothing happened, silent and willing co-conspirators. Before dinner, I managed to duck into my room to change before sitting down to a meal I barely touched. Sore all over, a warm bath offered little comfort as I gently poked at my chest, wondering if I had broken a rib. I blamed myself; I should have known better. I wanted to run away but knew I wouldn't get far. Who could I tell? More importantly, who would believe me? I was humiliated that he had fooled me and grew heartsick that he did it on purpose. From that day forward, I learned to prefer isolation and grew proficient at concealing what I could not yet understand.

Like that stray kitten, I grew shy and bided my time. Soon after that terrible afternoon, we all stood around my grandfather's grave to lay flowers and say a prayer in honor of his birthday. My mother rarely spoke of her father but this day she needed to reminisce. We sat around the kitchen table and listened to stories about a man who suffered from chronic asthma, worked in Richmond, fathered eleven children, and died when she was only nine. As I sat there with my milk and pound cake, I couldn't help but think that I was the same age when I lost my father; he just didn't die.

CHAPTER 4
MY ONLY ANCHOR

Nine is a curious age. I was still a child, yet shrewd enough to know that I was hopelessly out of place in my family. I would come home from Scouts and see Mom, Dad, and Robert playing *Yahtzee* at the kitchen table, laughing and joking about the life they shared. I was never asked to join the game; I wasn't part of their world. The happy trio of my mother, father and brother were a complete family unto themselves and needed no fourth member. More ominously, after my father's lesson in trust, I grew anxious that I was perceived as an intruder, who needed to be quashed in spirit, if not in body. If Mom knew what happened at the barn, she never let on, and I have never asked. So, when she told me I would spend the rest of the summer with her mother, I couldn't believe my luck. My grandmother's love and kindness delivered me from my isolation for two blissful months and I will be forever grateful. Our connection was symbiotic; she was my shelter, my little bit of normalcy.

In looks and manners, my grandmother belonged to another time. She proudly wore homemade clothes more suited to the 1930's than the early 1960's. I loved watching her brush and plait her long hair that lushly framed her face, then gradually grew thin and wispy as it cascaded down her back. She would wrap the long braid around her head like a halo, grab my hand and into the kitchen we would go to prepare my favorite foods: apple turnovers, beef with barley soup, and, my absolute favorite, chicken and dumplings. She'd cook up a whole chicken that would bounce up and down in the pot while she rolled the flour for the dumplings. My mouth watered all day as the food cooked on the stove. When it was time for me to go home, she'd pack up the food in mason jars, and every time I opened one of the jars, love would pour out just for me.

My grandmother had a round face with high blush cheek bones and brown eyes. The little lines, etched deeper by every smile that ever graced her pretty face did not diminish her beauty; rather, they were a testament to the pleasure she found in life. And she knew what it was to gather joy from the ashes. Sometime in the 1930's, during the Depression, she was suddenly widowed with eleven children depending on her. With the little money she had, my grandmother opened a boarding house near Williamsburg for a meager profit. It broke her heart to send her children as far away as Charlottesville until she could get her feet back on the ground. During these lonely years, loss piled on top of loss as her older children married and moved away. Her life and family would never, ever be the same.

Five years later, my grandmother found love again. She married a widower with one daughter, Eleanor, and moved to his potato farm on the Eastern Shore. Every year at harvest time, the Wise Potato Chip trucks would come up their driveway and one truck would have a big kettle of hot oil. They would go into Grandpa's fields and select a few potatoes, slice them, then fry them. If they met the company's standards, Wise would buy the entire crop and Grandpa, for a change, would sit in his rocking chair on the front porch and watch everyone else do the work. Those were the good years when Grandma would get a washing machine or a new sewing machine. If not, Grandpa would have to hire extra help. They would dig up 40 acres of potatoes and sell them at farmer's markets for much less money and far more work.

No matter if it had been a good year or bad, the entire family would always congregate every summer at my grandparents' house at the Eastern Shore. Cousins would come from Tennessee and Georgia to spend a week or two. We would lie in the fields looking at the stars, dreaming of our futures and creating our own constellations. Sometimes we would help out on the farm or in the kitchen, but mostly we ran wild, appearing only at mealtimes when we would eat field peas and tomatoes until our mouths were sore and our stomachs ready to explode. Then we stretched out on rocking chairs, talking about everything and nothing, while the adults looked on knowing these idyllic times were coming to a close.

After too many lean years and not getting any younger, my grandparents sold their potato farm to an attorney from New York City and bought a plot of land in the very rural Upper Peninsula.

They had waited a long time to build their dream house and didn't mind roughing it in their cramped Silver Streamline Trailer or using an outhouse (personally dug by my grandfather) while their new house was under construction. Their house was half finished when they welcomed me for the rest of my summer vacation, and I counted the days until the plumbing was up and running. I had heard too many tales of chickens pecking at bare behinds from under the crude plywood seat in the outhouse and snakes slithering over feet in the middle of the night. Of course, anything was possible; nights on the Peninsula were full of noisy active animals, but chickens? That was just too silly, until one night it became necessary to venture into the darkness, all alone, with a full bladder to the dreaded, stinky outhouse. I grabbed my grandfather's flashlight, its batteries strapped to the handle with electrical tape, took a deep breath, and hurried down the path, carefully placing one foot in front of the other lest I step on a mouse, rattle snake or the tail of a bobcat. The chatter of nocturnal animals and the faraway hoot of the owl in the moonless night sky made anything seem possible so I did my business as fast as humanly possible and ran all the way back to the trailer, not a chicken in sight.

One morning, while Grandpa helped the carpenters, Grandma decided to leave him to it and took me clamming on nearby tributary in their little tin rowboat. I cherished that time with her as I discovered a new world in the marsh with its distinct, salty smell and strange birds and insects everywhere. When we returned with enough clams for a tasty chowder, we were amazed at their progress, despite Grandpa's help.

By late July, and faster than I thought possible, the masons started constructing the house's brick façade and we were all itching to move in. The masons kept their six-cent reclaimed bricks in carefully constructed four-foot-high stacks. Despite implicit orders to stay away from the construction site, I found the bricks irresistible. I spent the next week building imaginary castles and ignoring the indignant chirps of displaced crickets. Cheerfully, I gutted the interior of each stack until only a hollow shell remained. Then I would construct a much taller fortress until I was completely submerged from the outside world like a king awaiting the enemy's approach. However, my success in building such an impressive barrier only succeeded in making me aware that I was alone, and lonely. Every time I heard the two-note, low to high, full octave whistle of a bobwhite, it seemed like the bird wanted to announce its presence to the whole world. Like the bobwhite, I sought to remedy my loneliness and called out to the neighbor next store. Distance was something foreign to me; I thought if I could hear the bobwhite, Woody, the boy next store, could hear me, too. I yelled, "Woody, Woody" at the top of my voice, but no one answered.

August arrived and so did the plumbers; the disgusting outhouse was finally history. Now, their new house boasted two bathrooms and proper plumbing, even if there was a hand pump in the kitchen and the toilets had pull cords for flushing. A rough and narrow path, assembled from bricks I had demolished in my short career as a fort builder, lead to Grandma's impromptu vegetable garden full of my favorite beefsteak tomatoes. Beyond her garden were patches of wild strawberries and blackberries where we ate more than we picked. Her flower garden contained roses transplanted from their property on the Eastern Shore; their gaudy colors and heavy perfume contrasted sharply with grandmother's demure mien. I liked to think that in another era she would have been a queen or conqueror, but, on second thought, maybe kindness is the greatest strength of all.

It was Grandma and Grandpa's fondest wish that this home would be the place where all their children and their families would congregate and enjoy each other for many years to come. They couldn't wait to entertain their family in the large living room that sported a fireplace and hearth that spanned an entire wall. Every chance I got, I would stand on the raised hearth and pretend I was Elvis singing to an adoring audience. One morning, after we had moved in, Grandma walked into house from her garden carrying late summer tomatoes when she stopped cold. "Don't move," she shouted to me as she ran out back out the door, the tomatoes forgotten, lying bruised and scattered on the floor. Wielding a hoe, she came back in the room yelling, "I know the smell of a black snake—watermelon. There's one in here." Sure enough, there it was coiled inside the fireplace. Grandma knew how to use the hoe and got the snake out without killing it. She carried the wayward reptile to the woods so it could find a proper home.

Grandmother, unlike my mother, loved animals. One day a hungry tom cat wandered onto their land and decided to stay. She affectionately named him "Tuptim" from her favorite musical, "The King and I." Never mind that the character of Tuptim was female; he was Siamese and that was close enough for Grandma. It was apparent that Tuptim was a citified kitty who distained our country ways, i.e. he had to catch his own supper. It was also clear to us that he was dumped by a family from town that no longer found him perfect. Tuptim had a crooked tail and Grandma believed this was due to a commonplace, but unfortunate, accident with a rocking chair that left the poor kitty to saunter through life perpetually signaling a right hand turn. I wasted no time in pointing out the obvious that Tuptim had big balls and a stinky butt. As my grandparents choked down their laughter, my grandfather explained that Tuptim's purpose in life was to breed with other kitties and if we got too close to him, he might stop, get lazy and fat. Despite Grandpa's decree, Grandma would sneak food to Tuptim and the other stray cats when she thought no one was watching. Every time I would catch her in the act, she would grow dearer to me as I watched her face light up as she tenderly ministered to these wild cats.

One day, while Grandma napped, I wandered off deep into the woods, my eyes skyward, fascinated by the contrast of blue sky against the deep green leaves, all the while remembering a teacher's stricture that blue and green did not go together, but here was nature proving her wrong. Nature demonstrated to me that not everything an adult said was true. Paying more attention to the canopy overhead than the terrain at my feet, I passed an abandoned farmhouse long reclaimed by nature. Suddenly the crunch of pine cones was replaced by a hard, dull thud as I lurched forward, catching my balance just in time as I stood at the edge of a large, forgotten old well with no protective barrier and camouflaged by years of overgrowth. It seemed that someone had improvised a well by digging a deep hole and carelessly fitting a wide terracotta pipe that just skimmed ground level. Bravely, I stepped close to the edge, ringed with slippery moss, and peered down into bottom of the well teaming with rank, stagnant water and nearly jumped out of my skin as a little brown salamander skittered over my sandaled foot.

I raced back to my grandmother, gasping for breath, and was surprised to find her still asleep. I made the fleeting observation that she looked tired despite her nap but persisted with my story followed by a multitude of questions about what animals lived in wells, what I could have held onto if the water was over my head, and what was it like to drown. I did not realize just how close I came to falling in that well and the ominous consequences. Though this experience became the stuff of many a nightmare, I have always trusted that Grandma would have come looking for me. I also sensed that I had a guardian angel from above to protect me. If I had been a cat with nine lives, I would have definitely been down to eight.

CHAPTER 5
SUMMER'S END

It was almost Labor Day. Soon I would say goodbye and return home to start school. Grandma and I walked to the little five and dime store where she bought me paper and crayons for the new school year. We went clamming once more, then stowed the boat until next spring. We shucked the last ears of corn and hulled the few strawberries that the rabbits didn't eat. Every afternoon before supper, Grandma read to me her favorite chapters of the Bible while I tried not to spill chocolate milk on the floorboards that were rough and bare until the arrival of Grandma's new gold wall-to-wall carpeting. I was particularly fond of the story about Jonah in the whale's belly, wondering how that could really happen. Lulled by the strong faith projected in her sweet voice, I wanted time to stand still, but each new day thrust me forward as if some unstoppable deadline had to be met.

Even nature seemed to heed the urgent call because autumn came early that year. Squirrels raced to stockpile acorns that dropped like little bombs on the driveway and roof of Grandpa's car. Overnight, the leaves seemed to change to yellow, crimson, and ochre, too eager, I thought, to embrace a long winter's sleep. On one of our walks, Grandma urged me to select a leaf and she would help me preserve it. I chose a strawberry red leaf, vibrant and soft. Betraying no sign of a blistering summer sun or wind-wracked storm to mar its shape, it was perfect. We hurried home and carefully placed it between two sheets of waxed paper wrapped in a towel and ironed them together. The scent reminded me of Christmas when Mom would light candles above the fireplace. Next, Grandma showed me how to make a frame with Popsicle sticks, and we decorated it with old buttons. I carefully packed this treasure in my suitcase to hang in my bedroom, a reminder of the ten months remaining, until I would return next summer.

On the last day with my grandparents, Grandma made my favorite breakfast: homemade buttermilk biscuits, Jimmy Dean sausage patties, and scrambled eggs with plenty of pepper and butter. I was skinny as a rail back in the day, and often accused of having a tapeworm, so no one minded if I stuffed my face with double and triple helpings. Grandpa kissed me goodbye as he left for work and blew a kiss to Grandma as she quietly sipped her coffee. Grandpa expressed concern over Grandma's lack of appetite because, in all the years they had been married, he had never seen her pass up a biscuit with plum jam. I was far too engrossed in my own biscuits to give his comment a second thought.

When I finally looked up from my plate, stomach ready to burst, I saw Grandma leaning back against the sink watching me - no - studying me like an artist studies an object he wishes to paint. Embarrassed by this attention, I made a silly face, Grandma laughed and shooed me out of the kitchen to play. Tuptim, forever at my grandmother's feet, yowled at me as I passed, swishing his crooked tail.

In the dining room, I grabbed the radio and flipped the dial searching for the heathen rock and roll station. As soon as I found Elvis, I lowered the sound and carefully positioned the radio so that, if discovered, I could quickly change the station. I was in nine-year-old boy heaven: a full stomach, rock and roll, and a brand new box of 24 Crayola crayons. I grabbed a piece of paper, took a pencil and filled the entire sheet with circles and scribbles which I colored with my new crayons. Humming along to "Return to Sender," I heard Grandma call my name. "Coming," I mumbled, continuing to color the scribble art and praying that I wouldn't be in Mr. Mackenzie's class. Nobody wanted Mr. Mackenzie because he gave homework on the very first day of school and even assigned a book report over Christmas vacation. I hoped my new teacher would be Mrs. Johnson, the other 4th Grade teacher. She was fun; she never gave homework over holidays and would always bring in candy or cupcakes for Halloween, Christmas and Easter.

In the middle of "Jailhouse Rock," Tuptim leaped on the table, sending the radio crashing to the floor. I shouted Grandma's name, wasting no time ratting out her feline miscreant's latest crime when I suddenly remembered she had called for me five, ten, maybe fifteen minutes earlier. Red-faced, I shoved Tuptim off the table, staring in disbelief at the wrecked radio and scratched table. I shouted my apologies only to be answered by the onerous tick tock of the hated grandfather clock that never kept the right time and chimed at odd hours all day and night. I found it strange that my apology went unacknowledged. I shouted my contrition even louder, adding that I would do the luncheon dishes and buy her a new radio out of my allowance.

Alarmed by the silence, I willed my leaden legs to walk from room to room, the only sound in that awful silence – the whine of her new refrigerator chilling an apple pie for tonight's dessert. I looked out the window at the empty garden. Her gloves and hat were exactly where she left them and the kitchen was tidy, everything in its place, except that she was not there. Now, cold hard panic seized my stomach, clawing its way up my chest, constricting it like a viper ready to snatch away any breath or sound that would bring her to me. I turned to walk down the hall to the bedrooms. The blood pounded so hard in my ears, I was deaf to everything, even the sound of my own trembling voice. I found my grandmother lying on the bedroom floor facing away from me. I stood there immobile as she struggled to turn to me, her eyelid and mouth drooping at the edges, mumbling for me to get help.

I didn't know what to do. Grandma didn't have a phone and Grandpa was still at work. I didn't want to leave her but I had to get help, so I ran as fast as I could to Woody's house three blocks away. The crushed oyster shells embedded in the concrete road cut my bare feet until each step left a crimson trail as I ran for help. When I finally reached Woody's house, I pounded on the door and windows but no one answered. A neighbor came out and roughly asked what I was doing there. I ran to him crying, tugging at the guy's hairy arm ,and just when he was about to turn his back on me, his wife appeared at the door in her housecoat. I looked at the wife plaintively; the only words I could get out were "grandma" and "help." The man bent down and took me by the shoulders and said, "Son, are you telling me the truth?"

"Of course he is," said his wife, who emerged from their house with her purse and cigarettes, spilling half of the pack on the sidewalk.

"Where do you live?"

"54 Magnolia Street. But we don't have a phone," I said, trying not to cry.

"Earl, call the police and meet me there. Come on, baby, show me who's in trouble," she said. I got in her car even though I was told never to get in a car with strangers.

The lady with the cigarettes ran into the house and asked me to take her to my grandmother. I pointed to the bedroom and the lady ran down the hall. She put a pillow under Grandma's head and laid a blanket over her to keep her warm. I stood in the doorway; Grandma's cheeks were so pale and her breathing labored. The lady put her arm around me and told me it was best if I went to the living room. I blamed myself for my grandmother's illness, my mother's disappointment; everything was my fault.

Soon two police cars with flashing red lights and sirens wailing roared up to the house, and four big policemen, guns strapped to their belts, hurried into Grandma's bedroom. Sharp commanding voices and the click and buzz of police radios filled the house as I retreated to the periphery, longing for one of the brick fortresses I had built that summer. The lady and her husband stood at the front door, smoking and talking to neighbors as my mother hurried into the house followed by an ambulance stretcher clattering down the hall and clipping a doorway, chipping Grandma's fresh paint. As she raced to her mother, I saw my mother quickly survey the house, finally locking on a trail of bloody footprints that pointed like little arrows to me. When the doctor arrived, Mom gently approached me, embracing me and assuring me that what had happened was not my fault. For the next week, I was relegated to the care of my aunt who lived in Williamsburg. She made coconut macaroons for me, and we sat down every day to watch *The Danny Thomas Show*. When Dad finally came to get me, he didn't say much—only that grandmother was in the hospital. The rest of the ride home was silent, but as I walked in the front door, I heard Mom crying.

"Dean," said Mom, "your grandmother has gone to be with Jesus."

Not wanting to understand what that meant, I shunned my mother's arms and went out back to my swing set to cry alone. My only anchor was gone and my life would pitch and bob like a rudderless ship on an angry sea. I was allowed to attend her wake and Mom walked with me to the casket. The room was full of flowers and my new Sunday shoes were slippery on the well-worn carpet.

"Can I touch her?" I asked. Without waiting for an answer, my fingers touched the ice cold, wrinkled skin of her arm. Mom gently pulled my arm away.

"She's so cold!" I said.

"Mom, why does she have her glasses on? Her eyes are closed and she can't see anyway."

Mom's face contorted, as she swallowed all the pain caused by my innocent remarks.

"Why are her eyes and mouth sewn together?" I persisted. "Look, there are stitches."

Mom turned around and said, "Robert, take Dean out to the parking lot for some air and we'll be there in a minute."

The next day, I found myself alone in our house with a babysitter I had never met before. Dad walked out the front door followed by Robert and then Mom looked at me and said, "You mind Peggy while we go to Grandma's funeral."

"But she's my grandmother, too," I said, not sure if I was more upset about being treated as a child and left behind or not allowed to see Grandma one last time and say goodbye.

"You're too young," Mom said firmly and closed the door. Faintly, I heard Mom say to Dad, "Poor thing, he just doesn't understand."

Pouting and feeling left out, I sat down to watch TV with this stranger and her five year old son. It rankled that I had to watch something as babyish as *The Shari Lewis Show*. I rebuffed all of Peggy's kind attempts to make this difficult morning easier for me. I doggedly flipped through the TV Guide searching for *Underdog* or *Superman*, until I looked up and saw Lamb Chop with his sewn eyes and mouth, just like Grandma.

Chapter 6
THE VEIL

I am back at that familiar creek, just at the edge of the Chesapeake Bay, where I spent many happy summer days clamming and crabbing with my grandma. The scent of brackish water transports me back to that treasured place of peace where my size 11EE feet are once again small and my little toes eagerly poke beneath the muck for the round-ridged shells of the sublimely tasty Chesapeake clams. Not sure of my purpose, I wade through soft, chest-high swells, happily splashing the water in sparkling arcs that turn to rainbows in the bright noonday sun. The foamy froth churned up by my play clings to my arms and chest, tickling me as the bubbles pop. I am surprised I'm so small.

Suddenly, I am in the middle of a sea change. The robin's egg sky is leeched of all warmth as twilight inexplicably ascends in a miasma of violet and gray. My breath is rapid and shallow as I scan the distant shoreline where the twinkling lights of faraway houses try to stave off the dark. The old red brick Chamberlain Hotel stands near the dilapidated southern terminus of the Little Creek Ferry I used to ride to the Eastern Shore. I hear the deep bass of the ferry's horn that stopped running 20 years ago.

The hulking white ship maneuvers toward the pier; I know whoever is piloting the boat has seen me and is setting course for me as I founder alone, waiting for rescue. Like a buoy anchored in treacherous water, I pitch and heave from side to side in a nauseating tempo as the ship gains speed. Its bow splices effortlessly through the towering white caps that jettison off its hull like fish trying to escape a predator beneath. Relentless, the ship bears down on me and I fear death lies in its wake. Desperate, I plunge beneath the water to wrench my legs free but they are bound like mooring lines, anchored to the bay bottom that abruptly falls away as my legs unspool in strands of malleable muscle and sinew, swaying in time with every eddy and current as my body plunges to the depths. Jolted by the release of an unseen hand, I breach the surface and brace for impact, but the boat slows down, its engines grinding in protest. The bay is now becalmed as if the boat's mere presence has stilled the waters. Curiosity transcends all fear as the familiar white hull trimmed in red and black turns again, this time pointing away from shore. This unknown, once-sinister vessel now imbues peace as it slows and comes near. I see an old woman directing the man steering the boat, his face obscured in shadow. She wears old-fashioned pointy glasses and her dress seemed overlarge. She is disturbingly familiar and is gesturing to me.

I see grandmother holding the rail, stretching her arm to me. I reach for her hand and delight courses through every vein as we touch. I am aware of piercing some kind of veil where past, present and future suddenly merge and are one. A strange sensation takes hold of my hand as plasma surges toward my heart. My vision clears as my heart fails. My eyes turn up into my head and I see the light. I am in it but I do not belong here; every ounce of my being revolts against it. I am not ready to embrace this journey. I must release her hand and it breaks my heart; does she know she was the best of my life so far?

The connection breaks and my surroundings come into sharp focus as the boat slowly moves towards the far shore, and I try to swim to her for one more glimpse of her lovely face. She remains on deck watching me but I'm still held fast to the bottom, tethered to life. I struggle to free my legs. Cursing at my failure, I look up to catch an impish smile crease her face and a slight shake of her head containing enough chastisement to put a fire and brimstone preacher to shame. Once again, I am a nine-year-old boy, naughty and busted.

I wake from this recurring dream thinking the next time I see her maybe I'll be ready with a coin in my pocket to pay the ferryman.

CHAPTER 7
SOLILOQUY

To this day, I could never explain in 20 words or less exactly how I survived. Let's just say that I had often heard that God gives you what you need. Several species of Australian frogs in the desert have been known to survive for several years without water. Those little brown and green bodies would go into a deep state of hibernation in a mud hole which eventually would turn into powdery sand. When it finally rained again, they came up and soaked up the bounty of nature, receiving enough sustenance to last them until the next rain. I doubt very much they thought about the next time it would rain. They were deep within themselves growing in their own way, the way nature intended for them to live.

During my childhood and adolescence, the occasional pleasant experience or humane comment brought me out of my self-imposed hibernation. But when the tides turned, and they always did, I retreated once more. I was always surprised by those occasional reminders of how the world saw me because I knew they did not see who I really was. I did not live where they lived. Just as I was sternly taught that blue and green don't go together, nature showed me otherwise.

Nothing is ever one-sided. My parents did pay for college and I became a successful businessman. With minimal support, my roots grew deep in the scant soil of a rocky hillside. I flourished and grew into a huge vibrant tree. I soaked up pure sun and breathed good air; all somehow supplied to me on my journey. I was privileged to see such trees on my many trips around the world. From the base of an ancient Mayan Pyramid in Guatemala, I climbed up to the top through elephant leaves, vines, and tree roots. It was virtually invisible from the bottom because of all the overgrown vegetation. I marveled at how they grew from nothing and then smiled. I knew this was a message. I always thought I was put here for a purpose but I never once thought of myself as privileged—far from that. My quest was to find out why I was put here. In fact, I have had jobs which have taken me to 27 countries. I learned something new in each one and somehow knew deep inside that the universe would be my teacher. I was a willing and able student. I know now the term is called "Earth School." It was something I would come to learn about in due course ...

CHAPTER 8
THE THIRD COURSE IS THE CHARM

New Year's Day 1990, New York City.

I was born under the sign of Leo, the sign of fire and nobility. Inside of me there was a lion waiting to be born.

However, for right now, I was alone in bed and could not find my glasses. I clenched my eyes against the sharp rays of a late morning sun as I blindly searched the nightstand and bedcovers to no avail, surprised, however, to discover a rather considerable erection despite what I had to drink last night. Too nauseous to even consider what would, on any other day, have been an obvious course of action, I staggered to the bathroom where a passing glance at the mirror revealed my glasses perched on top of my head. Two hours later and relatively sober, I shaved off my beard and moustache, shedding my first layer of protection with each drone of the razor. Welcome to the 90's.

Since graduating from college I had worked all over the world, and that had suited me because I was unable to commit to anything except learning about life. At first, exposure to so many cultures overwhelmed me when I compared my life to the people and customs of each country. In Indonesia, I arrived on a first class flight, checked into a five-star hotel where jasmine incense greeted me in the lobby. I traveled by chauffeured car to my office in a high rise building with tall glass windows and expensive furnishings. From my window, I saw a man living in a refrigerator box. His yard was a muddy river that flowed through Jakarta, hardly the typical riverfront property so prized in the States, yet, he smiled. Day after day, I was perplexed as I saw him smile. A light bulb went off in my head as if my guardian angel whacked me saying, nothing is all bad, or all good. My choices brought me to this well-appointed office looking through the glass, while a fellow human being endured a different experience, living by a putrid river in one of the most impoverished cities in the world. It was hard to watch this man not just survive but work his way through the circumstances of his life, enduring and coping *just like me.*

The universe had lessons to offer and I was ready for the next step. Like seedlings that grow strong despite the scant nourishment of a rocky hillside, I had managed to thrive in the barren soil of my childhood but I was tired of tallying old wounds. The truth was that I was lonely. I had doled myself out sparingly to the world with an eye always on the door, wanting an emotional or sexual connection but strictly on my terms. Needy, but unwilling to be seen perceived as such, I would deliberately turn away from people, preferring to come home to my den, my sanctuary, free of emotional turmoil. Breaching that disconnect would be a challenge.

My moment of truth came when I realized I had to dial a different area code in order to speak to a friend. For the past couple of years, I had watched so many friends pair off with partners and slowly spiral out of our circle. Two by two they wandered out of my life turning inward to explore the delights of new love, or worse, setting sail off the island of Manhattan to suburbia and all that awaited them there: *Baby Bjorns,* play dates and clothes that retained the sour smell of little bird droppings of spit-up, the new epaulets of the child-ridden. Being single had never really bothered me. I never doubted that I would eventually find "the one" until all my friends found theirs, and nothing says "nobody loves you" better than being relegated to the status of a third or fifth wheel. So I made the resolution that I would find "her" and, with any luck, the 90's would become the "us decade."

The bar scene soon proved to be fruitless. I eschewed dating services, and, as always, blind dates were an agonized waste of time. My parents were after me to go to church and find a nice girl but I didn't feel comfortable pimping God for a date so I signed up for a Progressive Dinner in Midtown. As nerve wracking as it was to walk into the restaurant alone, it would have been social suicide to continue with my solitary lifestyle. The knot in my stomach reminded me I was out of my comfort zone but I marched to that first table, sat down, and forced myself to talk. During the first course, I met Jane and Maureen, who were very nice but we had little in common. On to the main course, where I found trying to make conversation with

Carol and Helene as tough as chicken française placed before us. To make matters worse, out of the corner of my eye, I was alarmed to discover that I was in the sights of a blonde huntress. I was ready to bolt, when I caught a glimpse of an auburn haired woman, with curves in all the right places. Her name was Melissa.

As we nibbled a sinfully delicious chocolate and walnut cake, we exchanged pleasantries while "hawk woman" swooped in for the kill, depositing herself beside me, trying mightily to seize control of the conversation. As we talked, my eyes wandered to the cat brooch on Melissa's shoulder and the silver cat charm bracelet that tinkled on her wrist. Always a bit slow on the uptake when it came to women, I realized that sitting before me was a woman who obviously loved cats. Oh God, a man killer to the left and this crazy cat lady across from me. Just as I rose to make some lame excuse and hasty exit, I looked into Melissa's eyes and something in my gut planted me back down in the chair. I had found the green eyes that would hold mine for the rest of my life.

If one could see emotional chemistry, the air around us would have been filled with sparks. The blonde was forgotten as Melissa and I patiently waited out her trying prattle. As the dinner ended, the blonde hung around stalling to get me alone. I knew she wanted my business card, or worse, but I had no intention of giving it to her. Finally, when she didn't take the hint, I said goodnight to Melissa and left. If I had glanced back I would have seen Melissa's heart sink, and I would have never left her side. After the blonde left, I ducked back in and desperately searched the crowd, found Melissa and with my heart pounding, gave her my card. I'd journeyed from Tidewater to New York City and traveled around the world in order to meet my love, my hope, my dream. With any luck, I had reached the end of a very long journey; I had come home in my heart.

CHAPTER 9
JOSHUA, RUTH AND THEO

After meeting Melissa, I walked back to my apartment in Murray Hill realizing how lucky I was to live here. About three years ago, this beautiful rent stabilized apartment literally fell into my lap. A business associate was moving to Scandinavia and needed someone to take the apartment and assume his responsibilities as building manager for the landlady's two apartment buildings. I agreed, sight unseen, eager to get out of the hovel I lived in on the Upper West Side. Little did I know that my studio was just four blocks away from Melissa's apartment, so we may have passed in the street as strangers many times.

I knew this apartment was home the minute I stepped inside. Built in 1861, the building was originally a mansion owned by a prominent family and now it was divided into several apartments. The ceilings were twelve-feet-high and had three stained glass skylights that I discovered while removing paint left over from the World War II blackout. The walls were battleship grey with bright white trim. A marble fireplace sealed the deal because it was a great place to make beer with the best water in the world, straight from New York City's reservoir in the Catskill Mountains. Something began to settle in my bones. I always believed that if the struggle was too hard, it was not meant to be; life was meant to flow and this felt right.

Since I would manage her buildings, I knew I needed to take the time to get to know my landlady. I had been warned that Ruth kept close tabs on all her tenants, frequently waylaying them for what seemed like hours as she inquired into the minutiae of their lives and plied them with rambling accounts of her daily travails. I intended to invite Ruth for coffee after I had finished unpacking but she beat me to the punch. She called the very first evening and informed me, in a thick New England accent slightly north of haughty, that one of my first tasks was to bring her a selection of books from the lower level apartment where the last tenant had committed suicide. While she rattled off a list of obscure tomes, I thought to myself, great, what have I gotten myself into now?

For the next week I gave my cowardice full rein, sneaking past her apartment and dashing up the stairs to avoid this rather unsavory errand. A week later my manhood could no longer endure this spineless procrastinating and I trudged down the mossy stairs that led from the street to very small garden, cluttered with dead leaves and reeking of urine, just outside the basement apartment. I pushed open the heavy wrought iron door that quickly clanked shut behind me as I stepped into the dank, unwelcoming vestibule. Even on the sunniest day, it would have been a depressing and claustrophobic entrance into the world. I quickly unlocked the door, never dreaming I would actually be in a hurry to step inside when a blast of cold musty air hit me full in the face. Turning my head and waving away the invisible, I blindly explored the nearest the wall in search of a switch, only to discover the current had been turned off. Idiot, I thought, of course Con Ed would have turned off the electricity months ago.

I stood in the doorway, letting my eyes adjust to the darkness, when the last rays of sunlight slipped through the dingy, yellowed blinds and illuminated this sad place. The room was empty except for bookcases stacked to the ceiling, a leather sofa, and a coffee table. I wondered where he did it. I did not belong here with his possessions that no one had bothered to claim, the overturned flower pots, or the desiccated mouse so forlorn in the far corner. I heard no noise from the street, no music from upstairs; it seemed this space was out of sync with time as I knew it. I pulled out Ruth's list and quickly gathered her choices, well aware that this scant bit of light would soon be extinguished. Of course, the last book on her list proved impossible to find. I knelt down and wiped away the dust obscuring the names of some volumes when I sensed something watching me. The hair on the back of my neck stood on end, like a cat's whiskers when they perceived danger. The other side was here and I wasn't hanging around. I grabbed the books and ran for the door. As I walked up the stairs to the street, I chalked off the experience to an overwrought imagination until I passed another tenant who lived above the empty apartment.

"Man, you are brave to go down there," he said as he held the door for me. "Did you see the ghost?"

"No, just a dead mouse and lots of dust," I said, not really wanting to have this conversation.

"Some nights I hear banging, you know? I can't explain it. Hey, you look a little pale. Are you sure you didn't see something?"

"No, it's just the flu," I said and knocked on Ruth's door as my new neighbor fled to his apartment to escape the dreaded landlady. As I waited for her to open the door, once again, I wasn't sure if I was pleased or horrified that someone validated what I had experienced.

For someone who, supposedly, liked to police the comings and goings of her tenants, Ruth took her sweet time answering the door. Minutes passed as I waited, a bit rumpled, definitely rattled, and still peeved that I was sent like an errand boy to retrieve some dusty old books from a dead man's apartment. Finally, she opened the door, cigarette in hand, Sinatra on her stereo, and gave me the once over as she peered over black reading glasses perched low on her nose.

Like my grandmother, Ruth was elderly and fragile but the two women couldn't have been more dissimilar. If my grandmother was homespun, Ruth was definitely couture. Though the clothes she wore appeared dated, even I could tell they were fine designer pieces. She was meticulous in the application of her makeup even though deep-set wrinkles marred the final look. Her hair was dyed dark brown and pulled back into a bun that showed off her fine bone structure. Clearly, she still took great pride in her appearance and must have turned heads long ago. I don't know what she thought of me as I was ushered in with a wave of her hand.

I walked into her parlor apartment and it was like taking a step back in time to the elegance and ambience of a bygone era. Eighteen-foot ceilings boasted intricate designs in the plaster moldings, chandeliers hung in every room, and all her furnishings were museum quality. The parlor could have been the receiving room at Versailles but for the brown paper bags littering the parquet floor and a cat flicking litter out of his pan as he hunkered down to do his business.

"Joshua," said Ruth as if she was introducing royalty and no surname was required. With a flipping tail and slow blinking eyes, this overfed white Persian acted like he owned the building, not Ruth. She asked me if I liked Darjeeling, and, without waiting for a reply, poured the tea.

Sadly, Ruth had outlived two husbands and buried her only child after the terrible Polio outbreak in 1952. She was an acclaimed painter listed in *Who's Who in American Art*. During one of my first visits to her apartment, Ruth showed me a plant that burst its pot. She said she liked its tenacity in refusing to be confined by barriers. I believe Ruth wanted me to see that each and every life, no matter what form it takes, must break through to become what it was intended. Whatever barriers Ruth broke in through in her life, now, she spent half her day spying through the peep hole keeping an eye her tenants as she puffed on an ever-present cigarette.

But Ruth was a gem. The other tenants were missing something very special by avoiding her, and I was proud to call her my friend. We chatted endlessly about oil painting, and, when I told her I dabbled in still life, she encouraged me to try abstract painting explaining that abstractions sprung from the soul. Ruth said art was a snapshot of life and took me on a tour of her paintings showing that the art reflected in her portraits, still life, and surreal paintings represented periods in her life. Then she steered me to a three-by-four-foot canvas framed in a unique beaten down wooden frame. (In her day, Ruth was famous for the perfect frame selection.) I saw a rather large depiction of Christ on the cross, a conventional scene common in churches throughout the world, but the bottom of the painting caught my eye. Gathered at the base of the cross were people made from the same material as the cross, exhibiting every possible emotion, race, and creed. The blue and green stormy background created an incredible spiritual presence drawing me in, making me want to know more, see more, through the painting. My heart was full of questions as I turned to Ruth, who met my gaze with focus and wisdom.

"This is how you should paint, Dean, from your soul. You have talent," said Ruth, "but use your heart." She wagged her finger, "And light tells it all. How you use it tells the story on the canvas."

It wasn't long after this exchange that Melissa came to my apartment which had just fallen into my lap like Alice fell in the Rabbit Hole. With Ruth as my *Cheshire Cat*, who helped me to use my experiences in the building as a canvas upon which I began to paint my life. At first it was surreal, and then became more clear. I let in the light, and the effect was magical. When Melissa first set eyes on the building from the sidewalk, her face changed from smiling to frowning to smiling again. Taking her hand, we climbed the brownstone steps and I opened the double glass doorway guiding Melissa into the foyer. With a sharp intake of breath, she scanned the spacious entryway, the huge crystal chandelier, the red, white and gold wallpaper trimmed in dark wood and the checkered marble floor. When her eyes rested on the grand wooden staircase, she turned and quietly said, "I've been here before."

My reaction must have kicked her back to reality because she stumbled over words saying, "I mean, I've seen this place ... its *déjà vu.* It was a party, maybe a dream." She looked at me as if making a decision. "I was here with my friend, Sue, and we were having a party."

"Must've been a dream," I said and brushed it off. Walking up the stairs, I placed my hand on the small of her back to guide her as her eyes had a faraway look and she took slow, purposeful steps. When we entered the apartment, my fish tank greeted her with the graceful movement of colorful life covered in scales.

"I'm a Pisces," she said, smiling as if my owning fish and her being born under the sign of fish sealed the deal for continued interest. *I,* Leo the lion, was drawn to living fish, and *she*, the fish, was drawn to living cats. We were made for each other, I thought, and what she neglected to tell me was that the party she had dreamt about was a wedding reception.

The next time Melissa came over, she wanted to show me her culinary prowess and prepared a special meal of rolled salmon and cream cheese. But when we sat to eat, Melissa turned to the tank, grew queasy, and couldn't eat a single bite. This respect for my fish endeared her to me more. Melissa learned early in the game that, like a cat, I was grouchy if I missed a meal and scratched and made noises until I was fed. I believed Melissa liked me even more because of my cat-like behavior; even Joshua approved.

♣

As my life began to soar, Ruth began to decline. Less than a year after I met Melissa, Ruth was battling last stage lung cancer, and her family flew in from all over the country to say their goodbyes. When she was admitted to the hospital, I visited every day after work. One night, Ruth insisted on reciting poetry to me, but the strain was too much. I held her withered hand and stayed with her until she fell asleep. The next day, as usual, I set out once more to Mount Sinai. It was a cold, bleak February evening that made my sadness palpable, something you could breathe in to your soul. I walked in Ruth's room and found the bed empty. My stomach muscles spasmed, as if I had been sucker punched, and I fought the urge to wretch. I leaned back on the wall, slid to the floor, and cried.

The morning of her funeral, I awoke, reached to turn on the bedside lamp, and the bulb burst. Grumbling, I walked to the bathroom, flipped the switch, and the light blew. Shaking my head, I walked to the kitchen for a glass of water. Turning the switch, that light bulb blew, making the count three in a row in less a matter of minutes. Then I smiled: the light, *the all-important light.* Looking upward, I blew Ruth a kiss and knew she was saying goodbye in her own way, making sure I'd remember what she told me. February light holds a certain subdued hue. With the funeral in the dead of winter, the light passing through the front door of the building on the afternoon of Ruth's funeral, held a unique pattern in tones of grey and blue. As a burgeoning artist, I noticed the effects of light, and Ruth, the true artist, returned to me briefly through the sun's rays.

One year later, on the anniversary of her death, I saw the same pattern and hue of sunlight shining through the lobby doors. I smiled and understood this would be an annual event: a brief lifting of the veil between heaven and earth, and I was content to know that I was connected to her soul. I knew meeting Ruth was destiny and that our friendship brought love and purpose to my life. Ruth reminded me of my grandmother, the only stable force in early childhood and the only one who loved me unconditionally.

After the funeral, Ruth's nephew, Theo, told me that he wanted me to continue managing his buildings and be the "eyes and ears of his inheritance." We entered Ruth's apartment, and I walked softly as if I was treading on hallowed ground. As Theo closed the door, I saw a pattern of little scorch marks made by Ruth's cigarettes as she sat behind her door, day after day, waiting for news, waiting for company. As I struggled to maintain my composure, I heard her ask once more if I liked Darjeeling as Joshua jumped on Theo's lap. Theo told me that Joshua would now live with his family where he would be well cared for. He motioned to the room and told me I could take any one of Ruth's paintings. Without hesitation, I chose the painting of Christ, since it was Ruth's favorite, and because I had an internal itch for it, a *yearning*. Although this painting was unconventional, Ruth had taken the time to personally show it to me in detail.

"You have chosen well," said Theo, noting my selection.

When I looked at it, I was reminded of Ruth and the spirituality of life, like the "all seeing eye" described in *The Great Gatsby*. The painting was profound and unsettling, all at the same time, and I would treasure it always. Ruth's painting was now the centerpiece of my apartment. It always evoked a response; some even prayed before it, and one friend left never to return. Ruth would have been pleased with their strong reactions. I could hear her say "that was the sign of true art."

CHAPTER 10
D'ARTAGNAN

When we first met, there were only two cats in Melissa's life: Robin and D'Artagnan. When I was first invited to Melissa's apartment for dinner, the cats were as curious about me as I was about them. They were checking me out and marking their scent by rubbing against my legs. Maybe they smelled the fish food I fed my scaly friends and thought I was dinner. Perhaps they liked me, but Melissa disabused me of that fairy tale when she told me they rubbed their scent on people and things to claim them as their own.

As my lovely hostess poured the wine, d'Artagnan sat on the counter, moving closer and closer to the simmering pot containing a delicious marinara sauce with garlic and mushrooms. I didn't know it then, but d'Artagnan's favorite meal was spaghetti, so whenever Melissa made it, she had to fight him off as part of the process. When she walked to the refrigerator for the ingredients for a Caesar salad, the cats followed. When she threw something in the garbage, they went to check out their newfound bounty, then returned to their posts by Melissa. It didn't take long to notice that this scene was not confined to the kitchen. The cats went everywhere she went, and that included sleeping on her bed.

As a good guest, I offered to set the table. While placing the silverware, I decided that Robin (and its derivative "Binky") was a reasonable name, but where the *hell* did d'Artagnan come from? Who gives a cat such a ridiculous name? Three syllables, and a foreign name to boot! Was this an affected appellation to honor a French lover or, simply, affected? Either way, it bothered me but I didn't want to appear to be a crass Philistine. I suppose I could have simply asked her and found out that one of her favorite books was *The Three Musketeers,* but that would have been too easy and not the point. As we sat down to the first of many tasty meals we would share together, I plotted to change d'Artagnan's name. Loving a challenge, I broke the name down into its various components, d'Arta, tag, nan, trying to come up with an alternative. I thought, nan, on-yan, non, on-yon. "Onion"—that's it; much closer to one syllable and certainly less than three. And, it appealed to me to name a cat after a vegetable.

On my next visit, both cats languished under Melissa's chair, unwilling to relinquish their claim. "Onion" blinked nonchalantly in my direction, informing me that he remembered me and bore me no ill will. On the other hand, Binky barely exerted enough effort to show me his fat ass as each flip of his tail displayed more contempt than the last. He was letting me know, in no uncertain terms, that I was barely tolerated and I should watch my step. The cats were worse than any burly, overprotective father, but I realized that if I wanted to be close to Melissa, I had to be able to decipher their cues. An expectant look meant I am hungry, splayed whiskers showed interest, a playful chirp or threatening rumble deep in their chests conveyed emotion, and a sharp twitch of the tail meant get lost. I was learning.

Sitting next to Melissa I said, "When I die, I want to come back as one of your cats."

"Yep, they're lucky to have me," she laughed and leaned over to kiss me.

Emboldened by her kiss and ready to test the waters, I let loose my new name for d'Artagnan as he curled up at Melissa's feet.

"Onion, come here."

"Who is Onion?" Melissa asked with a perplexed look.

"C'mon Onion," I patted my leg to spur him on. "I think Onion is a better name than dar–tan-yon. It's easier."

"His name is d'Artagnan," said Melissa in a tone that implied I was crazy, stupid, or maybe both, but I was not to be deterred. Onion sauntered over Melissa's legs and curled in a ball between us.

"You see, he likes his new name," I said.

Melissa rolled her eyes. I knew I was pushing a boundary but I sensed Onion had to be his name. Onions have many layers, and I knew something was happening between us that would take time to unravel. Our bantering went back and forth about the cat's name for what seemed like months until one day d'Artganan pulled paper towels saturated with greasy bacon fat from the garbage, spattering grease all over Melissa's freshly cleaned floor. Her face turned beet red and she stared at the cat with dark angry eyes. I had never seen her like that before and neither had the cat.

"Onion, stop!" she yelled.

I was in shock; I couldn't believe it. She said, "Onion." I won! It was then that I realized I was beginning to have some influence in this relationship. A little fear struck my consciousness but was quickly replaced with laughter and anticipation of what would follow.

When it was safe, I said, "You see, Onion is a much better name. At least your subconscious knew that."

"D'Artagnan is a perfectly respectable name," said Melissa, "but I suppose it's okay for him to have a nickname."

I hugged Melissa, and we gazed into each other's eyes and connected in a new way. I sensed a power shift but knew she let me win. Our souls began to meld because of a cat, which, from that day forward, was permanently named after a vegetable. Somehow, I thought Onion knew I was responsible for his new name. I also knew the progress of my relationship with Melissa would entail a tug of war between me and the cats. Getting close to the cats would be a gradual process, a peeling back, layer by layer. Maybe that was part of what made the revised Onion moniker so appealing. In order to co-exist, we would have to get to know, respect, and accept one another, but I did not relish investing so much energy and effort in sucking up to these ridiculous cats because, if I was honest, I would be happier with Melissa without the felines.

Chapter 11
CHAOS

Soon dates became sleepovers, and sleepovers turned into weekends in each other's arms, which inevitably led to the shared notion that we should live together; in my place, of course. One thing, however, became clear; I was not a cat person. Though there were times in my youth when the idea of cuddling a soft kitten was irresistible; now, I could not shake my discomfiture. My fur ruffled at the thought of sharing space with two animals that didn't give a damn if I lived or died and would shed fur on everything I owned. Yet, here I am awaiting the arrival of my beloved and her two cats.

Before she moved in to my wonderful apartment with her destroyer cats, my Italian Renaissance Brownstone was a place of luxury with one occupant, me, and several happy, confined salt water fish. But even from her first visit, Melissa was not so enamored with one particular fish, a mean-spirited grouper that ruled the tank, constantly nipping at the other fish or worse. Whenever she stopped by, I came home to find grouper recipes from *Gourmet Magazine* or *Bon Appetit* taped to the refrigerator, subtle hints of my baby's displeasure. The other aquatic kink was the lion fish, a deadly beauty, who only ate live goldfish. So, when Melissa offered to feed them while I was away on a business trip I, initially and wisely, neglected to tell her it would entail a trip to the pet store to buy live feeder goldfish. Riddled with guilt, she poured the bag of goldfish into the tank and fled, returning after a reasonable amount of time to discover, to her everlasting horror, the sight of two mollies playing volleyball with the head of one of the unfortunate goldfish. Even though I heard about that for a week, my game girl decided to take me on.

The doorbell rang; she was here. I opened the door and the movers swaggered in with a ton of boxes. I grew pale and began to hyperventilate. Where would we put all this stuff? Did she really have all this crap at 76th Street? I already felt invaded. Melissa gave me a peck on the cheek (a portent of things to come?) and sallied forth into the night to retrieve her most precious possessions, Robin and d'Artagnan, I mean Onion. I started to sweat as I peered into the boxes containing a multitude of books, tapes, shoes, bras, and enough makeup, shampoo and conditioner for a year.

In less time than I thought possible to travel from Murray Hill to 76th Street and back again, Melissa buzzed from the lobby, and I ran down the stairs to help my girlfriend carry her cats to my apartment; no, *our* apartment. Why were my hands clammy? Was my vision really blurry? Was I having a stroke? At the bottom of the stairs was my darling Melissa beaming from ear to ear. At first, I thought it was because of me, but then I discovered she was so happy because her cats were finally here. I smiled, or it may have been more of a grimace; I don't know. Yup, everything's just great, I thought, as I carried the 20-pound Binky up the stairs as he farted sweet nothings and yowled at the top of his lungs. When I got into the apartment, I dropped the carrier on the floor and released the beast only to discover that the odor was not from a fart but a turd dangling from his tail. Melissa lunged for Binky, a wad of tissues at the ready, and remedied what would become the first of many feline faux pas. Leaving the chaos in my wake, I headed for the bar, passing the fish tank where the grouper was eating the angel fish. Home, sweet, home.

CHAPTER 12
YOU CAN LEAVE NOW

Battling the cats for Melissa's attention was a full-time job since she and her furry entourage moved in five months ago. I found myself doing unheard of things like doling out foul smelling cat food, which stank like a marsh at low tide; all that was missing were the crabs and we could have cooked those. I kept my mouth firmly shut and maintained the serene composure of a monk every time every time I wiped away their paw prints from my piano or vacuumed up the dirt from plants they had knocked over. However, I firmly drew the line at the litter box. *That* would be my honey's domain for all time.

Usually, Melissa was the first to leave for work and without fail the cats would be at her heels till she closed the door when they would disappear for a nap, or so I thought. One morning, I was running late (how do they know?) and the instant I opened the door, two blurs came out of nowhere and shot past me. One of the blurs ran upstairs, the other raced to the lobby. Damn.

The next morning, keen not to repeat yesterday's fun, I gathered my briefcase and coat, walked backwards to the door on high alert for the first sign of trouble. I managed to exit the apartment cat-free; as I turned the key in the lock, I heard the thunder of little paws racing down the hallway and the sound of the kitchen garbage can crashing to the floor. I knew those little furry bastards had declared war. What I didn't know was that the sound of a crashing garbage can would herald my departure from the apartment every morning for the next two years.

At work, I found myself fretting about the damage they were reeking on my once pristine abode. As much as I loved Melissa, I dreaded, just a bit, coming home, fearful of the carnage they had wrought. Every night, as I had done for four years, I closed the heavy, double doors behind me and I climbed the steps sheathed in thick garnet-colored carpet. Each footfall was softly cushioned, a welcome relief from the hard and unpredictable streets of New York. My hand traced the grooves of the heavy oak banister that was polished to a brilliant sheen and still retained its woodsy scent. The aura of the building seemed to say, here it is safe and comfortable; a perfect balance of style and nature.

Now the first thing to great me was the toe-curling stench of cat urine wafting from the litter box. And that was on a good day. If I was unlucky, my first glimpse of home would be Binky tearing away from the litter box, his belly careening from side to side. In the box would be a gift—a huge, uncovered, brown turd and I wondered if Melissa was hiding a German Shepard somewhere in our apartment.

Next, I would be met by a feline barricade blocking further access to my apartment and Melissa. My nemeses stood, shoulder to shoulder, tails swishing, scrutinizing me with menacing, bottomless pit eyes. I saw my father each time they glared my way. I secretly plotted to rid myself of these parasites but, for now, I knew I was helpless. Melissa had an unshakeable love for her kitties that nothing or no one could sway. In truth, I was envious of her attachment to Onion and Binky and hoped that one day her devotion to me would be as strong.

Sometimes I sat on the sofa with a scotch and I looked their eyes on a quest to search the mirrors of their furry little souls for something, anything: an emotion, a feeling, a spark of connection, a glimmer of recognition. Hell, I would have settled for a look of disdain, while hoping for an inkling of love, but the reflection always came back as a can of Fancy Feast. I knew some cats were capable of a love and devotion that could last a lifetime but I feared Melissa's cats were fully capable of walking over my dead body on their way to their food bowl, without a backward glance. Inevitably, the choice remained theirs, not mine.

All seemed well in our cocoon, until my Bible-toting mother called and Robin meowed loud enough for her to hear.

"What is that?" she asked, knowing I hated cats.

"Busted," I mumbled, then explained that Melissa moved in and so did her cats. Hell and all its fury let loose on the other end of the phone for my bold and brazen decision to live in sin. Melissa and I knew our only sin was laughing behind my mother's back.

When the energy of the universe drew people and things together, nothing could keep them apart. I was as magnetized to Melissa as she was drawn to her cats. As my mother tried to break our stronghold, I tried to stop the energy flow between Melissa and the feline beasts. I covered her eyes when an animal shelter commercial came on TV, or when we saw a sign saying "Free Kittens." I tried to cross the street before walking by a pet store. When I received a call from a friend asking for someone to take a free kitty, I ignored it, but resistance, indeed, was futile. Never having purchased a cat, they simply showed up in Melissa's life. I always envisioned a smiling vet every time Melissa walked in the door. I suspected that these cats filled a void in her life; she took care of cats because they loved her back. I kind of got it that the cats were never going to go away.

I thought about my past and realized that we were no different than a random proton and electron that had found each other floating in the cosmos, built exactly to relate and complement each other. The only logical next event would be for us to find each other and chemically unite to form another entirely different element which could never be split apart. Anyone who has taken chemistry knows that mercury, a toxic yet useful liquid metal, is only one proton away from being gold, a rare and valued element. It could only be logical that the chances of missing not only one, but several necessary protons in any relationship would be incredible great, yet as far as Melissa and I were concerned, we had come together and none were out of place.

I hugged her and burrowed in just like Binky would and said once again, "Melissa, I want to be one of your cats."

CHAPTER 13
THE BINK

In time, I found a growing, if grudging, affinity for the cats, though I never would admit it. The truth was simple; the cats' aloof nature reminded me of *me*. I have always suspected that was the reason Melissa was attracted to me, though *she* would never admit it. The cats held my eye through a luminous veil that suffered no dishonesty. They saw through me, my pain at the hands of those who should have loved me best, my cowardice that caused so many relationships to wither and die, and the willingness, at last, to love.

Melissa rolled over next to me, rumpled and cuddling close. Through half-open eyes I saw the cats adjust to Melissa's movement. They surrounded her in a shield of fur, her feline guardian angels. Propped on one elbow, Melissa's deep auburn hair fell around her shoulders. She reached over to rub my shoulder, scattering the cats. Her green eyes shined. "Are you alright?" she asked in a voice full of sleep. Not wanting to dwell on past hurts and needing only to focus on her, I brushed my hand over her cheek, then combed through her hair. Melissa leaned over and pressed her lips to mine. The magic and mystery of skin touching skin dissipated my thoughts of *veils*, cowardice and crashing garbage cans until *coitus interruptus* of the furry sort pounced between us.

"Go away!" I said through muffled kisses, trying to push the cats away. Melissa giggled and pulled away. Robin fell in a puddle next to her and she made baby noises as the cat leveled its eyes on me, as if to say, "I won, *asshole*. Take your party elsewhere." Breathing hard and defeated, I rolled over and gave Robin the evil eye. I swear that cat flipped me the middle claw as I came to the cold, hard realization that these cats came attached to the hip of the woman I loved. I had to get rid of them or find a way to make this work.

In high school French, I learned that "chat" means "cat." The lyrical sounding name in French reminded me of the past tense English version of something else, more like the deposits that greeted me from the litter box when I arrived home from work, causing me to nickname him "Stinky Bink."

One evening after a long day at work, I dropped my briefcase on the other side of the door and stretched to unwind. "Want a drink?" I asked Melissa on my way to the bar. Clinking ice into a squat, heavy glass, a glass made for a man, I poured two fingers of Maker's Mark while Melissa was muttering and clanging pots in the kitchen. I knew not to bother her so I slumped into my oversized leather arm chair and stared out the window.

The Bink casually wandered over, and with a loud trill, jumped on the arm of my chair and hunkered down, undeterred by a handkerchief thoroughly soaked with cat repellent. As this benign, obese sack of fur continued kneading, his claws softly pricking at the expensive fabric, I shook my head at the fruitlessness of any attempt to control these cats. As he settled in, still watching me, his claws retracted ... except for the big one in the middle. I sighed; at least the hanky kept the cat fur off my chair.

If I chose to admit it, there was something very special about the Bink. Listening to Melissa sing in the kitchen, I picked up the paper as the last merest kiss of sunlight shone opalescent on his coarse ebony fur like a drop of oil in water. Bink was beautiful. I picked him up and held him close to my ear, getting lost in the guttural purr that reverberated from deep within his body. The sounds and tones created an energy field that totally encompassed me. When I was in this place of heightened senses, the world seemed different, almost like I was on the threshold of something new. And then I looked up and saw Melissa.

"I'm going to bring the recycling down," said Melissa, not bothering to wipe the smirk from her face. "I'll just leave you two alone."

"Okay," I said, flustered and somewhat ashamed. I cleared my throat and unceremoniously dumped the Bink on the floor. I opened the window to cool my reddening cheeks, and the flimsy screen fell out, clattering two stories below to a deserted back patio. As I was wondering how I was going to retrieve that screen, out of nowhere, the Bink jumped up and walked out the window onto a small ledge.

"Robin!" I yelled in a hushed whisper so the neighbors (or worse,

Melissa) wouldn't hear. Mesmerized, I watched Robin's ease and confidence; his paws firmly connected to the six-inch-wide ledge with the forces of earth and no apparent fear of losing his footing. It was a connection foreign to my experience. He turned and focused his golden eyes on mine in a silent reprimand of what a fool I was for not believing in my own instincts. There was no way he was going to fall. The cat knew it, even if I didn't.

I lunged for him and grasped the soft fur covering firm muscles. My hands sensed something electric in his fur when I snatched him away from danger and promptly put him on the sofa. Knowing he was safe, my heightened senses reverted to normal and my heartbeat began to slow. It was as if Robin had brought me to the feeling of being on a ledge—knowing danger, but confident in your abilities. Maybe that's the threshold of the *veil*, I thought, a thin line that separates us from God and our connection with the universe. Maybe cats live on both sides. Maybe that's what they will teach me— how to be independent, but connected, to face my aloneness only by being with others.

Melissa came back in the apartment. She saw the screenless window, my face, Robin on the sofa and freaked.

"Was Robin on the ledge?" her voice held an ominous calm.

When I explained, she rushed to Robin, cooing to console him. In spite of the tension, or maybe because of it, all I saw was her perfect curves.

"He has electromagnetic paws," I said.

"Want to see a new move?" I asked, reaching my hand to her. She accepted and I pulled her to her feet. Turning her around, I leaned her back to my chest and begin stroking both sides of her face. "I call it 'the Bink'."

She turned to me, we kissed, and she said, "Close the window and let's continue in the bedroom."

"You're so easy." I said as I raced her to the bedroom. I decided to forgive Robin for his litter pan indiscretions as he had taught me a new and valuable move.

Behind the bedroom walls, our connection was electrical. When we were together, the light was on, and, when separated, there was darkness. I sensed a new journey budding in my heart, one that would open the universe to me in ways I never imagined.

CHAPTER 14
PARENTS AND CATS, TAKE ONE

Once we were settled, Melissa invited her parents for an overnight visit on Easter weekend, and the minute those generous words were out of her mouth, I knew she regretted the invitation. I had only met her parents twice before, and the little I knew of them, I didn't like. As zero hour drew near, Melissa fussed over flowers, arranged and rearranged pillows, and everything she took in her hands dropped to the floor, followed by a string of obscenities I had never heard before. Normally, I would have wasted no time teasing her, but one look at her told me this was no mere case of nerves; she was afraid. I had always suspected Melissa had been raised with the same cold hand and heart my parents wielded against me, but now, I feared, here was proof positive and thirty-six torturous hours lay ahead. When I opened the door, they stood before me in all their glory, petulance rising off of them like stink off road kill, and my dislike was confirmed. True to form, they roared into our apartment, prune-faced with anger, without so much as a "hello."

At first glance, Evelyn appeared frail and bent, dwarfed by a red coat two sizes too large. Though illness had plagued her for years, I feared her bones were infused with *adamantium*, our very own indestructible Wolverine, but without the moral compass. Large, thick lenses in her glasses overemphasized every emotion as she sized up our apartment and its inhabitants, searching for something or someone on which to vent her disapproval. Finally, her eyes rested on me and I felt the air being sucked out of me; she had her victim du jour, and I would quickly discover that I had met my first "emotional vampire." Melissa's father, James, was big and imposing, just like my father, and his bonhomie was a welcome relief from his wife's self-absorbed sulks. However, it took only one or two drinks and his persona crumbled. Raised up in its place was a blistering anger fed daily by his harpy's belligerence and the bitter, unresolved longing for the woman he should have married. The negative energy surrounding these two permeated the apartment, like one of Binky's turds.

"Get that moss off your wallet and buy me a cold beer." This was James.

"How can you live here? Traffic was horrible," said Evelyn.

Melissa's embarrassment was palpable as evidenced by her quick jerky movements and her refusal to look me in the eye. After a long bout of therapy, I knew by heart the "dysfunctional family cha-cha," one step forward and two steps back. Without asking, they shamelessly commandeered our bedroom instead of complying with the previously-agreed-upon sleeping arrangements i.e., a brand-new sofa bed. And we spinelessly agreed. They opened their suitcase and left it on the floor at the foot of our bed, and, as I went into the room to give them fresh towels, I noticed Robin sniffing around it, checking out the vile intruders. The next morning, Melissa and I were in the kitchen preparing breakfast when we heard her mother scream in the bedroom, followed by James yelling, "Melissa, get in here now!"

We ran in to find the "queen of mirth" and her sidekick, who were never short of biting words, now perfectly silenced and standing over their suitcase pointing to several, strategically placed, bear-sized cat deposits. I had to cough to hide my laughter, and Melissa ran to get paper towels. They didn't go to church, were gone within the hour, and everyone had salmon for Easter dinner. Karma is a funny thing, and our Binky was a willing agent.

After the litter pan incident, Robin and I forged a new relationship. He would jump on my lap, and I would give him my world famous jaw rub by facing him away from me and scratching both sides of his face. Occasionally, I touched his mouth but Binky didn't seem to mind; he used me for dental floss anyway. A grateful purr grew to a running motor as I whispered into his ear pretending Melissa couldn't hear,

"Bink, I know that I am asking a lot but just pretend you love Mommy for a couple of minutes each day. In return, I'll give you extra food and jaw rubs. But let's just keep this between you and me."

The truth of our newly forged bond was revealed about a month later when I returned home from a business trip to Paris. I walked in the door and I knew something was wrong; there was a pall in the air and Melissa looked downright dejected.

"Alright, who died?" I asked, not daring to hope that it might have been one of her lovelies.

"Robin refused to sleep with me while you were gone. He's your cat now, not mine."

While her conclusion was a bit dramatic and patently untrue, I was finally a card-carrying member of her colony.

CHAPTER 15
SAMMY

"What did you do?"

Melissa had just returned from her firm's retreat in the Poconos, carrying a blanket and wearing a big smile. I could always tell when she was hiding something—the guilty green eyes looking up under raised eyebrows were a dead giveaway.

"When we were leaving the retreat, I heard meowing coming from behind a house. When I went to investigate, there was a litter of newborns. The owner said that she hadn't seen the mother in days and was feeding them herself. I had to rescue at least one, so I chose Sammy because he had an injured sleepy eye. I didn't have the heart to leave him and take a healthy cat. He could have died."

"But why take any cat at all?"

She smiled, opened the blanket, and out popped a short-haired grey kitten, no bigger than my fist. Binky and Onion were immediately roused from their comas by the scent of the new kitten and decided to check him out. Feigning only a trifling interest, they gave him the once over. Sammy hissed, and Binky and Onion went back to sleep. Melissa scooped up her latest charge and informed me that Sammy resembled a Blue Point Siamese. Two big blue eyes looked up at me but the left was droopy and full of unsightly gunk.

"What about the eye?" I said.

She hemmed and hawed while I calculated the next vet bill but I had to admit he was a handsome little thing. Dark raccoon circles surrounded his eyes, and circles on his tail indicated a tabby somewhere in his gene pool. Rolling my eyes, I knelt to pet our new little one. Sammy immediately bounced up to me and sniffed my flip flops, then batted at my toes with his little paw, giving a hint of the strong, dynamic personality that was to come. He rolled on his back inviting me to play, and our bond was set; maybe this cat would be on my side.

His first night in our apartment, Melissa insisted that Sammy sleep with us. As we watched *Letterman,* I thought it was funny to wiggle my toes under the covers and watch the blankets move as he pounced and played. I vaguely remembered Melissa warning me not to encourage this activity, but as one o'clock drew near, I was half dead to the world and Sammy, of course, was wide awake. I rolled over and shifted my legs in a vain attempt to get comfortable and finally catch some zzz's, when ten tiny claws, sharp as any dental instrument, sank deep in my foot. I screamed as the comforter flew one way and the cat the other. "I'm bleeding!" Grabbing my foot and hopping, I saw razor thin, burning cuts that covered my foot and ankle.

"It hurts," I said as Melissa cleaned my foot with an antiseptic spray.

"I told you not to let him chase your feet."

"Let him? Every animal in this apartment does whatever they damn well please."

"Don't be such a drama queen; they're just little kitten scratches," she said, sticking out her leg and showing me her well-manicured foot. "I've got them. They'll fade in time. He's just being a kitten. Now go to sleep and try not to move."

"Thanks a lot."

A year later, Sammy was still shredding human flesh and I probably contracted Toxoplasmosis. A typical kitten, Sammy was full of life and curious about the magnificent things the apartment had to offer. He jumped on the toilet bowl rim and walked around and around, trying to lick the water until he fell in. Water splashed all over as the panicked kitten shot out of the toilet like a whiskered NASA rocket. Chunks of toilet paper were found everywhere, along with assorted pencils, sheets of paper, and unpaid bills, all evidence that Sammy had been there.

Sammy was like me because he had been adopted into a better life, just as Melissa and the cats had adopted me. Many times, Melissa caught me on my chair holding Sammy, petting his fine fur, lost in it. But there were days, like with any child, that Sammy's actions reminded me of what my mother must have felt. Melissa helped me see the humor in whatever Sammy did, just like her words and gentle humor helped me to see *me*. Thank God, I had Sammy's allegiance. Finally, I had something in that apartment to call my own. He loved to be lifted up to the cord that turned on the ceiling fan. He would bat at it for hours if I let him while I'd press my ear to his belly getting into the purr zone. I could suspend him upside down in midair or contort him into all sorts of positions without any repercussions, while Melissa got her arm chewed off just for looking at him the wrong way.

Living with "Mr. Personality" as I sometimes called him, was not always easy. Sammy's dark side reared its head from time to time when he would bite and not just a love nip. My reflexes were faster than his benefactress's, who was usually on the receiving end of his maladjusted nipping. Sammy would be quietly licking his paws, minding his own business, meaning, no humans need approach, when Melissa would walk over and reach down for a pet. In a flash, his jaws clamped like a vise but did she ever learn? *No.* After a long sleepless night, Melissa looked at me and said, "I can't take this any longer. I'm calling the SPCA." The white flag of surrender had been raised. Could this finally be happening?

"Honey, he's just being a cat," I said, silently kicking myself that I was more concerned with easing her predicament than giving Sammy the heave ho.

Melissa's frown lifted and her face shone with gratitude as the heavy burden of this decision was lifted from her shoulders. I hugged Melissa, holding on for dear life. I knew that vivacious, feral Sammy loved life and made every minute count. Yes, he was a handful, but most things worth having in life are. We continued to use the "He's just being a cat," quote to explain away Sammy's antics and I wondered why I chose to shoot myself in the foot.

I realized that my plan to get rid of the cats was not going to be as easy as I thought. My resolve was weakening; I was becoming attached. Little by little their claws pricked at my hard underside to expose a soft belly where feelings and emotions had been lying dormant, pushed inside and hidden from so many years of living with my parents.

Having the cats—and occasionally Melissa—around was still an adjustment for me. Last month, while I was on an urgent phone call with my boss, Melissa was in the kitchen singing, in a high falsetto voice an idiotic song entitled, "Sammykins, loves Mommy." Forget the neighbors; I was embarrassed my boss could hear but pretended I didn't and let him keep talking. When we finally hung up, I yelled to Melissa, "You make me so proud!" But my sarcasm obviously had no effect because shortly thereafter, she sang, "Sam I am a Ding Dong."

When I met neighbors on the stairs or in the hall, I would avert my eyes and mumble a greeting. I was afraid to meet their questioning, judgmental eyes, knowing they could hear every word of those stupid cat songs. One morning, Sammy and I showed up for breakfast, and Melissa burst into laughter covering her mouth and pointing to me and the cat. We both sported identical cowlicks or "tuffiness."

Life with our new kitten was never dull. After a day of apple picking, we brought home wonderful homemade cinnamon apple donuts. Cold and exhausted, we collapsed on our bed, too tired to move, when we heard a strange sound. We looked up to see a tabby tail moving backwards, followed by a Siamese-like torso and head with raccoon circles around his eyes with its teeth sunk deeply into a plastic bag full of apple donuts. We both laughed as we watched Sammy drag the entire bag of donuts from the kitchen counter to a destination only known to him. Our brazen feline was rechristened, "Sammy Bag of Donuts."

And like his brothers, Sammy had a fondness for human food. During one memorable breakfast, Sammy joined us on the kitchen table where he laid down, had a good long stretch and casually extended his paw, stretching it to a plate of buttered toast, gripping it with the suction of an octopus, and bringing the bounty close to his already "plus" size body. He was lazy, but smart.

♣

Melissa, caretaker and adopter of all cats male, took care of business first thing and had the veterinarian chop off their balls. This could not possibly bode well for me in the future.

"Male cats are more compatible than female cats, and all vets insist on neutering," said Melissa with a smile. "Better sleep with one eye open."

That was comforting. Sammy was the first cat we acquired together and I felt responsible for taking up his cause and preserving his manhood. The night before his "chopping," I brought the cat to Melissa in bed and said, "Mommy is going to have your balls cut off tomorrow! Yes, she is, and Daddy will do everything to protect you."

"You're not going to like it when he starts spraying everything in sight and this place smells like a skunk lives here," said Melissa, who was unable to grasp the importance with which a male treasures his ball sack.

"It already smells like a herd of elephants live here; what's the difference?" I shot back, stroking Sammy's silky fur. Of course, all my attempts to save the cat's manhood were for naught, and the next day, his balls were gone forever, but not before I watched in delight as Sammy scored points for ball sacks everywhere.

The minute the cat carrier came out of the closet, Onion and Binky made a mad dash for our bed and dove under to seek refuge in the farthest corner. Sammy, who looked like he would be easy pickings, managed to elude Melissa and joined his brothers under the bed. Undeterred, Melissa shuffled papers at the kitchen counter, drummed fingers, and waited ten minutes for Sammy to emerge before switching to Plan B. While singing one of her ridiculous cat songs in the hope of lulling Sammy into a false sense of security, Melissa crawled half way under the bed shoving a bowl heaped high with strongly smelling tuna as close as she could get to three pairs of laughing eyes. The fun really began when, all patience lost, Melissa's dulcet, sing-song voice grew shrill and I heard quite imaginative combinations of four letter words fly—and they were not LOVE, SOFT or CUTE.

A few days after the operation, Sammy jumped on the bed and tried to dig what was left of his claws into the bedspread, but couldn't get traction. The cat slid off the bed looking at me with eyes saying,

"No balls OR claws?"

And Melissa wondered why it was so hard to get a cat in the cage when it was time for a vet visit.

CHAPTER 16
The Engagement

We were randomly floating around in the cosmos until one event occurred that changed everything. Despite the cats, the fur and general chaos, I called Melissa's office after we had been living together just under a year. Without even saying hello, I said, "Grab a pen and write this down—Flight 874, May 10, Newark to Honolulu, 10 am, returning May 20."

Silence on the other end.

"You with me?" I said, my anxiety growing exponentially with each second only to be relieved by Melissa's resounding "yes."

Later that evening, Melissa told me that after she hung up the phone, she went into a vacant office, closed the door and had a panic attack. Everyone in the office knew about our relationship and people were taking bets on whether or not Melissa would come back an engaged woman. The day finally came as our jet taxied down the runway at Kennedy, and my only prayer was that we wouldn't run into any stray cats. As soon as we landed in Maui, I walked Melissa to a florist in the airport to buy her a fragrant lei strung with purple and white orchards. Hypnotized by the beauty and remoteness of this tropical island, the entrance to our hotel, the Maui Grand Hyatt, looked like a portal to another world. Bright yellow parrots watched our approach to the reservation desk, while glittering gold fish the size of salmon swam in small ponds beneath them. Due to the Gulf War, we received an upgrade because many people had cancelled their travel plans. As the bellhop escorted us to our room, Melissa raised her chin and pursed her lips; our suite was on the second floor and Melissa likes a view.

"I did not fly half way across the world to be upgraded to a room with *no* view," she whispered. I saw the hackles rise on her back.

"Pardon me, Madam, but your balcony overlooks the pool and the ocean."

And so it did; he opened the door to our spacious suite with a large balcony and an unobstructed view of the sky beyond it. There was a king size bed with more pillows than I have ever seen, a concealed television in a dark wood Chinese armoire, fresh flowers, champagne—the works. We walked to our balcony and saw vibrant yellow hibiscus and pink cottage roses, their scents in perfect fusion with the salty air. When Melissa expected the worst, the best thing I could do was to get her to chill and assure her that everything would eventually turn out okay.

"Are your knickers still in a twist?"

Melissa laughed but I was well aware that my honey came with a full set of claws all her own, and she was still annoyed that the bellhop had such good hearing. I had planned to propose that night at dinner but could not help but remember all the engagement horror stories I had ever heard. A tight knot wrenched my gut. On our one-year anniversary from the time we met at a restaurant in New York City, we found ourselves at the Swan Court in the Maui Hyatt. Having secretly arranged for our table with the maître d', we were seated at the best table in the restaurant which was located directly on the lagoon where beautiful swans glided over the water.

We watched spellbound as the red orange sky slowly subsided as a full moon rose into view. The dreaded anticipation of posing the question weighed heavily on me like kryptonite. As we were finishing dessert, I met her eyes and slowly withdrew the ring box from my jacket. She said, "yes." Meanwhile, an impatient couple harassed the maître d' demanding to know why we were taking so long. Our waiter told them we were getting engaged, and when word spread, glasses of champagne were sent to our table, while others actually stopped by and shared their engagement stories because they had actually gotten engaged there long ago. I smiled noticing that my beloved's attention primarily focused on the sparkly rock on her left hand. There could have been ten stray cats next to our table that night, and this is the one and only time she would not have noticed. We were even free of cat discussions for the entire evening; a record that has never been broken.

The next day we checked out of the hotel, hopped in our convertible and began a scenic, six-hour drive to Hana, on the other side of the island. As I drove, I watched the beautiful scenery while my shallow baby only had eyes for the ring on her finger. We discovered an arboretum halfway to Hana and strolled through a primeval forest of bamboo. The tall green stalks swayed in a gentle breeze as the sun broke through in long, fractured streams of light. The only sound that quelled the unearthly silence was the intermittent chirps from the birds rocking above us in the soft fronds of bamboo. I picked a pink and white orchid and tenderly arranged it between the crook of Melissa's ear and her soft auburn hair. I cupped her face in my hands and kissed her softly as the bamboo cradled our bodies in softly dappled light till I felt something crawl up my fingers.

"What's crawling all over your face?" I said to Melissa, obviously irked that my grand romantic gesture was infested with mites.

As hard as it was to leave this place, we continued the drive through some of the best scenery I had ever seen including tall lush mountains boarded by the vast ocean with scattered palm trees, verbena, bamboo, tall pink ginger flowers and pineapple. In the midst of this grand, romantic paradise, we turned to each other and lamented about leaving our cats at home and cried in unison, "Poor Onion!" On every trip, Melissa would choose one cat to worry about and this trip's lucky winner was Onion. She was just like my mom who would stew about cleaning her immaculate house during our family vacations. As we pulled up to our destination, Melissa said, only half joking,

"You suckered me in by giving me this ring in the lap of luxury of Maui Hyatt and then dump me in this rat hole state park that costs fifteen dollars a night?"

Yes. The state park was rustic with tin roofs, picnic tables, and bunk beds. But it also had black sand beaches, caves to explore, and I thought it would be romantic. Melissa grumbled all the way into the hut, plopped down on the skimpy mattress, grabbed her Walkman, and frantically started searching on the dial for some sign of civilization. The New York gene still had full rein in my sweetie's psyche as she prowled the cabin, disgusted with everything she saw, until she spied a box of Friskies with a note left by the previous occupants instructing when to feed the mongooses. "Oh look!" she said, content as a lamb, and it didn't matter that they weren't cats.

We began to look for a restaurant and soon discovered that the only one in town was at the world class hotel, the Hana Maui. Since we were scheduled to stay there the next night, we headed for town. We finally found a small country store, similar to a 7/11, with less than 20 food items in the entire store. Somehow, we managed to gather a box of pasta, marinara sauce, Italian salad dressing, iceberg lettuce, a couple of tomatoes, and Maui onions. We went back to our tin roofed chateau, grabbed our bathing suits and beach shoes, ready to explore the scenery.

Though there were four other shanties in the area, we had the whole place to ourselves. There was a reverence about the place, like you were in God's cathedral and silence was the rule. Where else could you hear the waves and wind, birds and animals conjure a hymnal all their own? It seemed disrespectful to talk. Winding our way through the purple bougainvillea and wild ginger, we finally came to the little cove with a black sand beach, obviously pumice from volcano ash and thousands of years old. The sand was more like granules of sharp rocks, and we were happy to have our beach shoes. For a city girl who, two hours earlier, had been griping about this place, Melissa led the charge as we explored the beach, rocks and caves.

Back at our hovel, I watched Melissa nesting, happily engaged in preparing our dinner. The pungent onions were crisp in the salad and the marinara tasted like it had been prepared at The Culinary Institute. It was as simple as you could get and the best meal we have ever eaten. Sometimes simple things that were taken for granted in New York or even frowned upon were magical here.

That night I kept Melissa close, just the two of us secluded in paradise. Magic. Until a torrential downpour hammered our tin roof sending me to a Zen-like blissful state and Melissa to, once again, fiddle with her Walkman, unable to banish the worry that the only road out would be washed away and we would be stranded, never to see civilization again. I tried to talk some sense into her but Melissa possessed a set of invisible antennae with the sole purpose of honing in on problems that didn't exist. Since sleep was now impossible while "Miss Doom and Gloom" tossed and turned, I went to pee. I walked in the dark to the bathroom and turned on the light only to be greeted by what looked like a maneating roach. It was half the size of Manhattan. I grabbed the trash can and crushed the unwanted visitor.

"What's going on?" she called, sure that I had dispatched a burglar.

"Nothing dear," I said, my voice rising higher than I would have wanted. Since I had just calmed her down about the rain, I had no intention of introducing any new issues but I knew Melissa wasn't buying my story so I nonchalantly returned to our bed, kissed her goodnight, and rolled over. I could still feel her eyes burning a hole in the back of my skull as I fell asleep.

As promised, the next day we checked into one of the top five hotels in the world, the Hana Maui. It was like having a five star religious experience in our own private bungalow, complete with a fenced in front yard, perfectly manicured one-inch-deep grass, a front porch, a bathroom built for celebrities, a bamboo poster king size bed, and everywhere I looked, there were orchids. Naked and not caring who saw, I jumped in the Jacuzzi on our private lanai, thrilled that there would be no mites or roaches or anything else to worry about that night.

The next morning we rose early to take a dip and since no one else was there, I looked into Melissa's eyes, held both her hands and sang, "What do the Simple Folk Do?" from *Camelot*. It was good to see her laugh again, and for the remainder of our vacation, we did everything imaginable, including helicopter rides and snorkeling from a catamaran off an atoll. I will never forget the sight of Melissa clinging to on the side of the boat wearing a full life jacket until she was shamed into releasing her death grip on the boat by a 5-year-old boy who swam by with nothing but a swimsuit. Maybe she was part cat after all. The clear azure water was chockful of beautiful Naso tangs, butterfly fish and a myriad of other species we couldn't hope to name. They swam together in graceful harmony and when it was time to return to the boat, I couldn't get Melissa out of the water. It was funny how letting go seemed so hard but when you did, the entire world availed itself to you.

We spent the last night of our Hawaiian trip at the Pink Palace in Honolulu. Melissa looked at me and said, "We can do this again when we come back."

"Well, we're here now, and there are no guarantees we'll be back," I said, thinking of Ruth, who always said to live in the here and now.

All too soon, it was time to leave Hawaii. I hated to see the sadness in Melissa's eyes but knew it knew it was because this was the best time she ever had and not just because of her ring. Just before we boarded our flight, when no one was around, she hummed softly, "Black Bear, Noir Bear, Je t'aime le black Bear" and I knew she was preparing for reentry. However, before Melissa left, she had to have one last taste of guava juice. Distracted and looking at me, Melissa pulled the tab and the beverage erupted all over her white top. Her eyes warned me not to laugh, but it was impossible. I doubled over, barely able to breathe, while Melissa swore under her breath saying something about divorce lawyers in New York.

Melissa huffed off in search of a new top and her dignity, while I wiped the tears from my eyes hoping she wouldn't ditch me. As we boarded the plane, I whispered that since this was a red-eye, I doubted anyone would have noticed anyway. Melissa just glared at me and handed me the bill for her new top. As the plane ascended into the night, she announced, apropos of absolutely nothing, that when she died she wanted her ashes brought here and scattered in the Pacific Ocean. I supposed that this declaration was her idea of an olive branch but I understood her heart. This was the place where we were engaged and where Melissa had felt more at home than anywhere else.

Upon our return, all three cats stood by the door reeking of their kittysitter's perfume, an obvious sign that they had been deprived of all affection in our absence. We sighed and resigned ourselves to a spate of being cold shouldered. What Melissa and I didn't suspect was that prior to our arrival, the cats had held a secret conclave which determined that Sammy would be the instrument of our punishment. That night, while we rested snug in our bed, sleep being out of the question since our internal clocks were whacked out, Sammy began playing on our pillows. At first, we welcomed him, clueless to his real purpose, and chastised the other cats who fled to the hall. Sammy began climbing the beautiful oil painting hanging over the bed. It was a large rendition of a wave done in various shades of grey and white with soft brush strokes of pale yellow. I was particularly fond of this painting, now that we returned home with memories of sunlit waves crashing on a black sand beach. Realizing that we had been played for fools, but too close to sleep to fight it, we let them have their revenge as Sammy played all night on our heads, bouncing off what used to be a beautiful painting. Did I really hear snickering in the hallway?

CHAPTER 17
THE ANNOUNCEMENT

The next weekend we drove to Central Jersey to see Melissa's parents, Evelyn and James, to give them the great news in person.

"Dean and I are getting married!" said Melissa. "Mom, we have so much planning to do!"

Not missing a beat, her father said, "You two go on plan your own wedding and leave us out of it because we're not going to pay for it. Just tell us where to show up and we will be there."

Melissa's mom nodded in complete agreement as I watched Melissa look from one parent to the other in disbelief at their callousness. Dumbstruck, Melissa and I excused ourselves to go outside and get some air. We decided to cut our visit short and drove home in silence. Melissa looked out the window and wiped away the occasional tear. Sometimes, I knew Melissa better than she knew herself. All she wanted, in the world was for her parents to be happy for her. This would be the kind of reaction you'd expect to receive from your average mother and father but her parents were not typical people. Evelyn and Jim were damaged by illness, addiction, and, probably, abuse. As a consequence, they chose to inflict it on others or, perhaps, they just enjoyed being mean. That was the hardest thing for Melissa to understand, that love did not conquer all. She had excused their behavior for years, chalking it up to a vast litany of rationalizations, but now she was finally beginning to understand that they did, indeed, have a choice. They chose to belittle her generosity, deny her the dignity of respecting her person, and threw her newfound happiness back in her face.

As we crossed over the Hudson into Manhattan, the skyline of New York shown like a beacon in the night guiding us home. I felt like I had passed through a wormhole into another dimension where lives were healed and reborn, despite those whose mission in life was to cause pain. So we would proceed with our wedding plans by ourselves, with a minimum of magical thinking.

We awoke the next morning with all three cats sleeping on Melissa's side of the bed, and I marveled at how she could stand it. Binky was curled up like a crown above Melissa's head, *bogarting* most of her pillow, Onion nested between Melissa's legs, and Sammy was velcroed to her left hip. I looked at her and all her cats and I began to understand the connection. They were like band-aids on the wounds inflicted over the years by the two people who brought her into this world.

CHAPTER 18
TIMMY

How foolish I was to think that three cats were enough in a one-bedroom apartment. As Melissa tells it, she stopped for a slice at Mimmo's Pizza on Fifth Avenue after a meeting with our minister to discuss our wedding plans when, *all of a sudden,* a poor, tiny kitty creature with matted fur and a twisted neck hobbled its forlorn body to where she was sitting, minding her own business, and clung desperately to her ankles. She reached down to gently pet the kitten, and its plaintive meow sent her maternal instincts into overdrive. Melissa gently coaxed the timid kitten into her eager grasp, and, with the skill of a veteran diplomat, chatted with the owner about the kitten's history and convinced her to surrender the kitten into her custody so she could take him home and get him proper vet care.

Later that afternoon, I opened the front door totally unaware of the new encroachment on my peace and slumber. Minding my *own business,* I discovered our bathroom door had been barricaded, again. Why? After the normal "How was your day?" pleasantries, Melissa came clean and I put my foot down.

"Four cats? In this apartment? The litter pan overflows as it is. How much is this going to cost?"

"I don't know, his appointment is tomorrow, maybe $300?"

"That's just to walk in the door; try $1,000. We're talking worms, mites, fleas, a twisted neck, and tests for Feline Leukemia and AIDS."

"Wow," said Melissa with all the sincerity of a cobra hypnotizing its prey. "You're really becoming an expert on cat care."

I was so taken aback at her flaccid attempt at flattery, I couldn't even respond.

"You're right," said Melissa, knowing she had left the pall of truth far behind. "I'll call the cat shelter tomorrow."

I don't know if I was more amused or offended that she would think I would buy such a blatant lie. Melissa had caved in too readily and seemed too happy to have seriously entertained the thought of giving up Timmy. Did she really think I was dim enough to believe that she would spend all the money necessary to restore this cat to health and then give him away? I suspected the pizza joint was probably glad to get rid of such a pitiful excuse for a mouser and had cheered them both out the door. So, with nothing else to claim our attention or finances in the months preceding our wedding, we took on this sick little kitten as we kept up the charade, every night repeating the same lines. A month later, with no sign of Melissa relenting or Timmy leaving, I surrendered.

"Did you call the animal shelter?" I asked for the last time.

"I did," she said, with eyes as wide as nature would allow and cheeks pink, the dead giveaway.

"And what did they say?"

"There's no room, not yet. I was told to call back after Christmas."

"Whatever," I said. "Let's just keep the fur ball."

So, Timmy became our fourth cat, and Melissa's seventh rescue. Plucked from adversity, this woebegone kitten eventually evolved into a healthy beauty with thick fur, a sweet disposition and a very long tail that unfurled into a bushy question mark. When he walked toward you with his tail posed and his neck still slightly bent, it looked like he was always was in a pose of perpetual wonder.

The newest member of our family was warmly greeted by Sammy, who kicked the crap out of him every chance he got. Of course, Timmy's fur was so long and thick that Sammy's teeth barely grazed skin. Frequently after pouncing on his brother, Sammy would walk away shaking his head in disgust, trying to spit the long fur out of his mouth. Eventually, Sammy calmed down and occasionally we would catch them grooming each other. When that happened, we knew all is well with the world.

In the time leading up to our wedding, I learned many valuable lessons about my bride to be: Melissa should not be let off the leash to wander at will or, at the very least, not without a keeper at her side maintaining a constant vigil. On the other hand, Melissa had just saved Timmy. I looked up on the wall at the painting of Christ. For years I had always thought there was only one Savior in my apartment and it was hanging up prominently on my wall but that is when I realized that I had two. Melissa was the savior for many cats but also for me. She had taken me under her wing, or should I say paw.

I may never fully understand her mania for cats but I did make her promise, no more than four cats. *Ever.* Four was my absolute limit and she agreed. However, I didn't intend to stop trying to become the king cat. Now, we have a closed society consisting of six souls, not all of them human, living in my apartment, so let the drama begin.

CHAPTER 19
MY ABLE FELINE ASSISTANT

All that was once foreign was now beginning to have a sense of normalcy. Just like the first night she made me dinner, when I watched in awe as Melissa multitasked around the cats, I learned to do the same, and it took some getting used to since any interaction I had with my fish was definitely one-sided. Now, there was nothing unusual about a cat perching on my shoulder while I fielded calls about pigeons on windowsills, no hot water, or the time a movie producer called because he wanted to film the streams of roaches pouring out of a hole in the wall in one of the buildings during a renovation. I particularly liked having the cats around when hostile tenants called to complain of mice, "What are you talking about? I live here and I don't see any mice." Each tenant issue was discussed with Theo during our daily conversations. Laughing and sharing these stories developed our business relationship into a great friendship.

At the beginning of every month, tenants slid their checks under my door, and I recorded the deposits in my small office, a cubby hole, really, near the front door. The office was furnished with the usual business accoutrements: a phone, computer, printer and a large, ornate wooden desk that someone had discarded near my old apartment on 75th Street. With a little sandpaper and varnish, not to mention my sprained back thanks to lugging this monstrosity up two floors to my apartment, the banged up but inherently beautiful desk, was restored.

It brought me back to childhood and my little desk that had been passed down through generations of my mother's family. Every day, I would sit behind my little desk that was covered with the names of previous owners scratched into the surface. With my crayons and paper, I pretended to be a big shot executive issuing orders over an old phone my father had liberated from the shipyard. Even at age four, armed with bright primary color crayons, it gave me the confidence to know I could go out in the world and make my mark. The archives of my experiences resonated when childhood dreams were fulfilled. At the office, as well as at home, I was finally sitting behind a real grown up desk, dealing with grown up issues like complaints about roaches. Okay, so that's debatable, but as I connected the dots in my somewhat chaotic universe, I experienced the full-circle effect; I realized that everything must have a purpose. I was here for a reason.

A few months after Timmy dropped anchor, several of the tenants suddenly stopped paying their rent. When I called to inquire, they told me they had slipped the checks under the door like always and I must be an incompetent fool. Confused, Melissa and I searched the small office. Finding nothing, we waited until the next month's checks were due and watched as Timmy pounced when a check slid across the floor. He bit the corner and, with his head held high, walked directly to the piano. With one swipe of his paw, Timmy made a deposit. Even after the little sneak-thief was caught red-handed, Timmy still jumped on the desk pawing through my inbox looking for checks. Thus, the missing check mystery was solved while another emerged. Why was Timmy only attracted to checks?

"Don't overthink it," said Theo, never short with words of wisdom. "The tenants will get over it. Let them mail their checks if they can't get a sense of humor."

Just when you are sure it can't get any worse, we returned late one Sunday evening, dog tired from a weekend in Woodstock, NY, and opened the front door. The ammonia-heavy smell of cat piss rocked our sinuses. Fighting the urge to gag, we searched the usual places: litter pans, a pile of unread *New York Times* but didn't find anything. The fumes persisted despite our efforts to uncover the source until we finally traced it to my in-basket, which now had truly lived up to its name. All Theo's documents, mail and the buildings' checkbooks had been given a golden shower. But who was the stealth pisser? There were four candidates but our suspicions were confirmed the next day when, while I was working at my desk, Timmy brazenly prepared to squat in my new inbox.

CHAPTER 20
A CHRISTMAS TAIL

Two weeks before the wedding and all the ensuing madness, Melissa decided to surprise me with a special celebration just for us. When I returned home with bagels and orange juice, my favorite Funfetti cake was already in the oven and Melissa was in our closet-sized kitchen making lemon curd for the filling. As I poured the coffee, I luxuriated in the delicious aromas of vanilla cake and citrus wafting from the kitchen. As Melissa worked feverishly whisking and humming, an overwhelming feeling of love and wellbeing permeated our home. And then, as if on cue, Timmy jumped on the counter and startled Melissa, who lost her grip on the bowl. It tottered on the rounded edge of the sink and then tipped the wrong way, spilling half of its contents down the drain.

I heard words I never thought would come out of Melissa's mouth, in combinations that piqued my interest. When I chuckled, she shot daggers at me, daring me to laugh. I handed her another cup of coffee with a shot of whiskey and tried to look contrite.

"Funfetti is my favorite cake, even without the curd."

After taking a sip, Melissa eventually lightened up and carefully carried the two layers on cooling racks to our travertine coffee table in the living room. Melissa returned to the kitchen to try to salvage the remaining curd, while Timmy followed his nose, jumped on the coffee table and began gnawing at the hot cake. Steam spewed from its center as Timmy broke it open and took a bite. This was the first time we ever saw the cat eat. Melissa ran to shoo him and I learned a few more words. When the smoke cleared, there was a gaping hole in the side of my cake.

"I give up," my darling declared as we headed out the door to buy our Christmas tree. Before I closed the door, I scanned the apartment, knowing that when we returned, things would be askew. True to form, before we had even locked the door, the garbage can hit the floor with a dull thud and I even didn't want to think about what was happening to my cake.

Descending the brownstone's steps, we walked arm-in-arm, the smell of roasted chestnuts and blaring car horns filled the spaces between bustling pedestrians. As we weaved through the crowded sidewalks, we enjoyed the best face of the city—a New York Christmas. Stopping at the nearest tree stand, we lifted and shook the trees, trying to decide between a spruce and a Frasier Fir. We decided on the Frasier, Melissa's favorite, and began to haul its eight feet of ungainly limbs back to the apartment.

After backending the tree through the door, we wore out three chef's knives trimming branches and whittling the trunk to fit into the stand. Finally, the tree was up but looked puny and dwarfed by the 12-foot ceiling. Obeying my darling's wishes, I got on my knees and wrestled the tree over to the window for the *perfect look*. D'Artagnan jumped on my back to swat at the branches that were swaying around my head. I tried to shake him off but he dug his claws in deeper.

"Get him off of me," I said.

"Come here, baby," she cooed, but not to me, she was talking to the damn cat!

"Yes, I'm fine. Thanks for asking. I hope you can get blood out of my shirt," I said, still on my knees trying to turn the tree when I noticed that the more I turned, the more needles fell to the floor.

"Dammit! We got skunked by the salesman."

Tears welled in Melissa's eyes as her Martha Stewart moment quickly faded.

"The damn tree is a dried up piece of crap," said Melissa, as I took her in my arms and tried to console her.

"It's really not that bad. See, only the bottom limbs are shedding their needles," I said as I twisted a marginally supple limb to and fro, demonstrating my sincere and overwhelming desire not to drag this tree down two flights to the street, argue with the salesman, and drag another tree back home.

"Oh, all right," sulked Melissa who, between the curd, the cake and the tree, was too tired to argue. As I held her and stroked her hair, I was the epitome of concern and understanding. Inside, I was doing my happy dance but not for long. Perhaps she sensed my mood, (after all she was a Pisces) or maybe she was thinking up new arguments so that next time I hauled another damn tree into the apartment, I could permanently injure my back. Whatever was on her mind would remain forever unsaid because Sammy, bless him, chose that moment to jump into our box of ornaments.

We hastily agreed that if we wanted to salvage our ornaments we'd better start decorating this dried up, husk of a tree *now*. I opened boxes of twinkling lights while Melissa picked through the remains, explaining the protocol for decorating a tree when there are cats in the house: put the expensive, sentimental ornaments on top and the cheap ones down the bottom. Easy enough, I thought, but as I placed my first cheesy ornament on a lower limb, Timmy walked over, enthralled at the new glittering plaything, and, with one swipe of his paw, shattered it into a million pieces. After sweeping the shards into a dustpan, I swore off the baubles and took the box of tinsel Mom had sent me and began to drape it, strand by strand, in the famous Parker family tradition. Melissa gaped and snatched every bit of tinsel off the tree, horrified at my ignorance and convinced my mother had planned to kill her cats, which is just the kind of thing Mom would do, upset Melissa and have me pay for it, literally. With funereal *gravitas*, Melissa explained the concept of "tinsel tail" - how tinsel goes in one end of the cat and gets stuck on the way out the other. Since this would be quite hazardous to the kitties as well as my wallet, I threw the tinsel in the trash along with my family's tradition.

Two hours later, we were admiring our Christmas tree and grateful that the ordeal was over. While I tidied up, Melissa took a long bath to get ready for her bridal shower. On the bed was a new dress from Sak's and her, first-ever, pair of Manolo Blaniks. While she primped, I watched the football game until I heard a shriek and saw one shoe fly out of the bedroom. Apparently, one of her darlings had hocked up a particularly mushy hairball in her treasured shoe. The day I had been waiting for was here and my hands were clean! They had gone too far, even for my honey because, I hoped, such a disgusting transgression would surely usurp any bond of affection. I cautiously approached our bedroom, the sullied shoe in hand, and my heart sank. Melissa was nuzzling the culprit. She snatched the shoe out of my hand, wiped out the offending matter, and slipped the shoe on her foot. In an instant, I knew the cats could do anything, including murder, and she wouldn't care. Grabbing her coat and keys, Melissa said, "Time to go!"

"Have fun and bring home lots of good stuff," I said, kissing Melissa as I relished the delight on her face. Robin, of course, blocked her way to the door to get one last bit of attention before she left. As Melissa leaned down to pet Robin, Timmy ran past and jumped on the piano. He flicked his tail a little too close to the pine-scented candle and, like a match, it caught on fire. Melissa sprang into action. She was careful not to spook Timmy, who was heading straight for our tree, which was nothing more than tarted-up kindling. Thank God, his tail was so fluffy; he didn't even know he was on fire. In seconds that actually seemed like hours, Melissa lunged and clapped her hands on both sides of his tail snuffing out the flame. The fur on his beautiful tail was now crinkled and charred as Timmy sashayed on.

"Ignorance is bliss," I said, and, when all was calm, I walked Melissa to the street.

As the yellow heap pulled away, I stood in the street watching the tail lights fade, just like my earlier life. My world was expanding in all directions and I wanted to pull it in to get control, to get back to myself. But I wanted Melissa, who came with chaos standing on sixteen furry paws.

Stuffing my hands in my pockets, I turned and trudged up the steps. My breath fogged my glasses but my purpose was clear. This was asinine; the cats had to go. It was me or the cats. I had enough already with tails on fire, hairballs in thousand dollar shoes, and fur on everything I owned. Stomach churning, I opened the apartment door. My home reeked of burnt cat fur, which almost drowned out the horrid stench from the litter box. Sammy was sitting on the sofa giving himself a bath. Even from down the hall, I could hear a rumble of discontent from deep inside his chest. He left his paw in midair as he glared at me, his ears flat against his head and his eyes big and black. D'Artagnan, fresh from hocking up the hairball, was burrowing in the kitchen garbage can. Timmy jumped on the bookcase sending my vintage lava lamp crashing to the floor and Robin sat perched on my chair, his fat bulging around his haunches, flipping his tail back and forth like a ticking time bomb. All four eyed me, trying to see what I was made of and if I had the guts to take them on. I stomped my foot and said, "En garde."

Chapter 21
PARENTS AND CATS, TAKE TWO

I remember the first time we visited my parents in Virginia; we lost our muffler somewhere on the New Jersey Turnpike, and, by the time it was replaced, we didn't arrive until 3:00 a.m. Exhausted, I carried the suitcases to my room and didn't bother to unpack. We were to separate rooms, of course, and Melissa, barely conscious, just grabbed a nightgown, robe and whatever she we needed to wash up. On her way to the bathroom, Mom stopped Melissa in the hall to ask what she'd like for breakfast. Somehow, Melissa got her second wind and sat with Mom at the kitchen table talking with great energy about everything and nothing, all the while gesturing with her toothbrush and toothpaste. I went to bed.

The next morning, Melissa knocked on my door.

"Last night, I was talking to your mother and waving this around," whispered Melissa, her cheeks bright red as she showed me a tube of Ortho-Gynol Contraceptive Jelly.

"I thought it was my toothpaste."

Mom never mentioned the tube and chances are she didn't notice, but the memory for me will always be priceless. Now, it was their turn to visit us. The wedding would take place in two days, and my parents had arrived early for a pre-wedding "Welcome to Hell" overnight visit before checking into their hotel. I secretly suspected my parents were here to break up our impending union, since they hated coming to New York. However, my parents frequently visited Robert, often traveling to Minnesota, Kansas, Florida, and upstate New York, but who's counting? We both believed that society designed all this pre-wedding agitation to test the couple to see whether or not they could survive the actual marriage. I could tell Melissa was nervous because she couldn't stop twirling the rings on her fingers.

I think back to a spiritual leader who explained that a log must be in the fireplace in order to have a fire. She instructed that if each student took themselves out of the situation, then there would be no energy left to burn. If not, the pain of the fire would endure until you learned to stop it. Early in my life, I constantly obsessed about what I should say to them. Before each visit I would practice how to protect against their attacks but all this was wasted energy because they were masters at their game. The secret was to simply detach, and with that, the door buzzer sounded the warning that my parents had arrived.

"This should be interesting," I said, passing Melissa on my way to the door.

Grateful that the cats were nowhere to be seen, I welcomed my parents to the den of sin I shared with my fiancée. Dad had a "greet the preacher" smile plastered to his face, Mom didn't even bother to feign happiness, and I knew this was going to be a long, long night. After some brief hugs and hasty kisses, Melissa ushered my parents into the living room where the dreaded felines lurked. I hung up their coats, and, once more, hopped on the hamster wheel to nowhere.

Like Evelyn, my mother was small in stature; she looked frail but could deliver a punishing kick. Though her fingers were dainty, she had earned her living by typing and sewing. Until her retirement, Mom was employed as the top secretary for a senior vice president in a telecommunications company. Her favorite story was one that illuminated her rigid code of righteousness. One day the phone rang and her boss told her to tell the other party that he was not at his desk. She firmly told him that she was a Christian and could never tell a lie; she pushed the phone button and said, "He will be with you in just a minute." She was so straight-laced, no starch was needed. With every inflection of her premeditated disapproval, your weaknesses were brought to light as if examined under a microscope. If she did not deem you worthy, there was no winning. Dad was more subtle; his babyfaced, southern good 'ol boy act concealed a bully's heart. Anyone in tune would pick up the falseness; especially a cat.

We planned in advance to serve hors d'oeuvres at our apartment before dinner, so Mom and Dad could relax while we caught up.

Melissa placed an assortment of cheese, bread, and fruit on the coffee table; she offered my parents hot tea or coffee. I poured us some wine.

"No thank you, we ate at LaGuardia," said my mother.

"Can't we offer you something?" asked a stunned Melissa, who, despite all proof to the contrary, still expected our parents to be polite and play fair. I didn't need to see her face to know she was hurt. I could hear it in her voice which had lost its ebullience, turning quiet and flat. I was certain their behavior was about something more than the trivial matter of coffee or cheese. They knew Melissa was anxious to be a good hostess, and my parents, particularly my mother, were not about to give her that opportunity. They would rather stuff themselves at an airport greasy spoon and have the pleasure of flinging a monkey wrench at what should have been a lovely evening.

"No, we are fine," said Mom.

It suddenly dawned on me that the reason they would not accept anything we offered, besides purposefully insulting Melissa, was because of the cats. My mother probably thought we had sprinkled kitty litter over everything and maybe we should have. Once Melissa recovered, she proved to be a pro at salvaging any situation. Growing up with an alcoholic father had taught Melissa, at an early age, how to finagle herself and her parents out of a myriad of awkward situations. I glowed as I watched her shift into high gear chatting about our nieces and nephews, always a safe and successful topic since my parents practically converted one wall of their living room into a shrine with countless photos and mementos dedicated to their first born and his brood.

While Melissa steered the conversation, I took a deep breath and debated if another glass of wine would ease the surging headache behind my eyes. For the present, I tabled that decision because I shouldn't leave all the work to Melissa. I turned to speak to my father but he was flipping through the pages of *Newsweek* with great conviction while a "do not disturb" vibe emanated from his every pore.

Thank God, Timmy and his little pea brain decided that our soiree had become far too boring and something had to be done. Totally guileless, Timmy meandered over to my parents, rubbing up against their legs, swirling his tail this way and that, depositing long, white fur all over their pants. Not to be outdone, Onion sat by the fish tank, hind legs splayed, licking his ass with great vigor. Just when I thought the evening couldn't get any better, Sammy picked himself up and moved with great deliberation out of the room, down the hall to the litter pan. Melissa and I exchange horrified looks as all conversation ground to a halt. Everyone heard him scratching his way in the sand and then emitting a hearty stream of urine. When finished, Sammy jumped on the kitchen counter in full view of everybody. I glanced over and saw my mother's face contorted as if she was gagging. I laughed as I remembered that this was the same woman who used to interrupt our childhood vacations to clean her house.

"What's so funny?" asked Dad.

"Nothing," I said, reaching over to snag a piece of Maytag Blue that my parents were obviously not going to touch. I believed they would have sat there and died of dehydration rather than taken one sip of our water or tea. While I poured Melissa and me another glass of wine, headache be damned, I wondered if my parents knew how many roaches lived in New York City, including the hotel they were about to check into tomorrow.

"Before we go to dinner, I have a little present," said Mom, handing Melissa an early Christmas present wrapped in green and red plaid paper, topped with a gold bow. Well, now I felt guilty; perhaps they weren't so awful after all. Melissa beamed as she kissed my mother and carefully unwrapped the present, her cheeks pink with anticipation. The gift my mother selected for her new daughter-in-law was a small but beautiful Lenox box. As Melissa profusely thanked my parents, a small piece of paper fell out of the box and fluttered to the floor. Melissa picked it up and silently read it. A hot anger flared in Mom's eyes, supplanted in the next breath by an air of benign ignorance that was unimpeded by the slightest shred of embarrassment.

"Oh, thank you … thanks," Melissa stuttered, handing me the paper. It read, "A Special Note from Lenox. Thank you for buying our exclusive One Time Collection Set. This is your free gift as our token of appreciation for your purchase."

In a spectacular display of understatement, Mom waved away any need for gratitude, and I went back to the bar and polished off the wine. I wasn't driving and I didn't care. I handed Melissa a slice of apple with some Montrachet and asked Mom if she was sure she didn't want something to eat when I saw Binky jump on top of the sofa, his eyes trained on Mom, ready to execute the coup de gras. Binky moved with casual menace, his belly swaying from side to side, and I wondered how such short legs could gracefully balance so much weight. The Bink was on a mission. With each step, his nails softly plucked the fabric of our new sofa and for the first time that evening I was enjoying myself. As Binky walked behind my father, who stoically ignored the cat and his wife's discomfort, Melissa assured my mother that the cat just loved people and wanted to say "hello." I knew Mom wasn't buying Melissa's excuses as her back became ramrod straight despite the beginnings of scoliosis. As she monitored Binky's progress, her eyes flitted back and forth so rapidly I thought she was having a seizure. By the time Binky got to Mom, she was so tight and rigid I could have used her as a surfboard. Binky's face was a study in cool disinterest as he stretched his front legs, then his hind legs, as he eased his large, freshly groomed, spit-cleaned body on her shoulders and carefully curled his tail around her neck. Binky even had the nerve to nestle close, sniffing the cologne she had dabbed behind her ear. Well, that did it; Mom sprang to her feet, her arms flailing in a useless attempt to rid herself of every stray strand of cat fur, and I knew it was time to go. The barely displaced Bink promptly went to sleep, and I hustled everyone out the door; never mind we would be a half hour early. Clearly, Binky wanted to teach Mom a lesson; perhaps that middle claw was not so bad, after all.

The four of us were a jolly sight as we rode up Park Avenue in dull silence. Even the cab driver gave up trying to initiate a conversation after just a few blocks. He must have thought we were going to a funeral. I tried to catch Melissa's eye but she just stared out the window, and I knew she had grown weary of being the dancing bear in this miserable circus. The prospect of two more hours of forced, inane conversation and fielding insults to my future wife and the home I loved was intolerable. As we entered one of my favorite Italian restaurants, *Il Vagabondo,* I realized I would have been far happier at home with a tuna sandwich, if it meant my parents were not going to be there. Well aware that our wedding loomed in two days, I searched for some way to see us through the rest of this evening. The only thing that saved the night was the delicious food; it certainly wasn't the torpid conversation. Once again, my parents only came alive when we discussed Robert and his family. On that topic, and only that topic, we were in complete agreement: Robert's children, Julia, Rachel and Adam, were beautiful inside and out. When the check came, usually I would have reached for it but decided to enjoy watching Dad squirm. He ordered more coffee, asked for more water, and played with his spoon, while I sat on my hands until he reluctantly picked up the check. It wasn't my proudest moment but it felt good; clearly both sets of parents had declared war on our forthcoming marriage.

That night, with my parents safely tucked away in the living room, and *Letterman* running down another "Top Ten" list, unwanted memories began to surface like bubbles in a glass of champagne. It was my brother's wedding day and I had just returned from a swim in the hotel's pool when I heard my Mother ordering hamburgers for lunch from room service. I quickly showered and dressed and about twenty minutes later, there was a knock on the hotel door. Yea, lunchtime; I was starving. Mom, who was dressed in a pretty yellow gown trimmed with white lace and faux pearls, opened the door and the waiter rolled the white linen draped cart into the room. I felt like I was a celebrity. I marveled at the polished silver covers on each plate. This was a special occasion for my family and we were going to do everything right. My mother handed a plate with a burger to my father, my brother, and removed her cover with a flourish. When I asked for my burger, Mom looked at me and said, "I forgot to order for you and there is no time now. Don't worry; there will be plenty of food at the reception."

Even if someone offered me a bite, which they didn't, I wouldn't have been able to swallow it. How could anyone forget their own son? I remembered my father boasting to me that the Great Depression was rough but that he never went without a meal. As crazy as it might sound, I never lived through the Great Depression and I *did* miss a meal!

Suddenly, I heard Melissa say, "Why don't you say something to them?"

"Because they'll make a scene and that's exactly what they want. Honey, we love each other and that's all that matters. Our parents never wanted us to be happy as children; why would they want us to be happy now?" We needed to remember that.

We turned off the light, and Sammy snuggled in my arms after he was booted out of the living room. I listened to him purr and was at peace. I pondered the change that came over a cat when they saw a bug or a bird: their tranquil muscles tensed, fur stood up, eyes widened as their body assumed a stalking pose. In a heartbeat, I could be holding a predator; the dichotomy of the cat's behavior was difficult to understand.

"How could this loving animal kill other animals?" I whispered.

"It's hard to believe," said Melissa, "until they are proudly sitting at your door like a Viking home from his latest spate of carnage, a dead mouse hanging limply between their choppers, their chests puffed out in pride, shoulders squared, whiskers splayed and their eyes searching yours for the expected round of applause for a kill well done. Even then, you still love them."

In the morning, we bid my parents a brief adieu as they pulled away in the yellow cab. I remembered the back of their Oldsmobile pulling away after dropping me off at college. I was just as happy to see them leave now as I was then, but this time, I was much stronger. Yet, I felt cheated because I knew, unequivocally, nothing would ever change. The past would never be redeemed and we would continue as we always had, but now they could inflict their bile on Melissa, too. I hoped that any interaction with my parents at the wedding would be short and sweet, if I was lucky.

CHAPTER 22

THE WEDDING

Today was our wedding day and here I sat, all alone, hyperventilating in a small, stuffy room at back of our church. My groomsmen had deserted me a half-hour ago to escort an array of elderly aunts down the aisle leaving me in this sparse room with nothing to do, nothing to read, not even a Bible. Pacing, I strained to hear the beautiful music I had personally selected and was missing as I sat abandoned in this hole while everyone else was having a good time. I knew Melissa was ensconced in the church's elegant bride's room being fed bonbons by her adoring attendants. After all, I was *just* the groom; all I had to do was buy a tux and show up.

As I wallowed in nerves and self-pity there was a quick knock and the door flew open. A clerk hurried in and shoved papers under my nose for my signature. I stumbled to the desk, nearly missing the chair, took the pen in my shaking hand and signed away my bachelorhood. If anyone had seen my signature, they would have sworn I had the DT's. Embarrassed, I pulled myself together and thanked God that I had found Melissa . . . and her cats.

Soon there was another knock on the door, I jumped and a disembodied voice announced, "Its time." We entered the sanctuary. The roses and lilies were beautiful, their scent almost overwhelming. I saw the altar with a large cross, and images of Mayan human sacrifice flashed in my brain. Still, I meekly followed the minister to the altar as I felt all eyes on me. Unnerved by all this attention, my shoes were suddenly the most interesting thing I had ever seen. By now, my knees were shaking so hard, I didn't know how much longer I could remain vertical when (Hallelujah!) I heard the processional. I turned and saw Melissa; thank God, all eyes were now on her. Radiant in her white gown, holding a bouquet of roses, lilies, and stephanotis, Melissa owned that aisle and no veil could obscure her happiness as she walked to me and our future life together.

Prior to our wedding, Melissa and I had agonized over the anticipated and much dreaded behavior of our parents in front of friends and co-workers. A friend, who understood our concerns, presented us with a very unusual wedding gift, "The Automatic Bullshit Deflector." Simple to operate, you merely placed both hands over your navel and took a deep breath and, viola, an invisible and impenetrable shield would rise between you and whoever was trying to dole out misery to you on your wedding day. We had not used the "ABD" yet and now that the ceremony was over, I thought maybe, just maybe, our parents would be intimidated by the whole New York *thing* and we would emerge unscathed. However, our beauties had different agendas and did not disappoint.

As our guests left for the reception, the bridal party, as usual, stayed behind for photographs. As the photographer snapped away, the bridal party smiled, relatives who had flown in from all over the country smiled—everyone smiled except the mother of the bride. We did not realize how bad it really was until we got the proofs back and saw Evelyn, like a malevolent Mr. Magoo, glowering at the camera in every photo. Fortunately, on the way to our reception, Melissa and I polished off a bottle of Perrier Jouet in the back of the limo and didn't give Evelyn a second thought. By the time we arrived, we were a little buzzed but no worse for wear and happy to discover that the party had started without us.

As we twirled around the dance floor in our first dance as husband and wife, Julia and Rachel, who were our adorable flower girls and little Adam, our ring bearer, danced around us. Before dinner was served, the band leader called for the father of the bride to toast his daughter and her new husband. Our guests looked around waiting for Melissa's father to rise, but our Jim, for reasons known only to him, refused to stand and toast his daughter. Thank God, a prescient uncle, who clearly had experience with Jim and his petulant impulses, stepped in and saved the day. I squeezed Melissa's hand, willing all the love I had in my heart into that one, simple gesture. She smiled and pretended all was well but I saw her play with her earrings, a sure sign that she was upset. Even as loving friends and family raised their glasses to our happiness, Melissa struggled to shake off the sting of her father's boorish stunt. I would never forgive Jim for his spineless and failed attempt to derail our reception and embarrass my wife.

After all the champagne and upset, Melissa and I were starving. When our guests had been served the first course, my father rose, as planned, to lead the blessing. He was well-spoken and devout in his faith, so I was pretty sure he would rise to the occasion and not screw it up. Somehow, he managed to concoct the longest, most rambling and boring prayer I have ever heard. Just as I, and everyone else, hoped the end was in sight, he delivered the kicker: "And, Lord, give this couple as much help as you can because they are going to need it." I have never been less proud of anyone in my life. Amen. Once again, I had foolishly given him my trust and jumped, only to end up on the barn floor, embarrassed and hurt.

Nothing mattered now as everyone ate and drank. Like many couples, Melissa and I were so busy greeting our guests we missed out on most of the food at our reception, only to eat our own wedding feast of Cheerios and chamomile tea at about three in the morning. The warmth and love we experienced on our wedding day from true family and friends more than recompensed for the boorish behavior of three sorry individuals. It was truly bittersweet to say goodbye to far-flung family who you only see at weddings and funerals but we looked forward to having brunch with many of them in less than ten hours. We ended our wedding day as we began, at home. I carried Melissa through our threshold and over to the bed.

"Get me out of this thing," she mumbled, face down, her shoes in her hand, and I foolishly assumed there was some hot sex in my future. No, that would have to wait for morning. We spent the rest of our wedding night practically in a coma watching reruns of fifties and sixties TV shows on *Nick at Nite* until we fell asleep in each other's arms, our furry children nestled around us. Whom God Hath Joined Together, Let No Cat Put Asunder.

CHAPTER 23
OSCAR

We all have been told that the center of our solar system is the Sun but any cat owner knows better. The center of a cat owner's universe will always be the cat, like the sign of Leo which has always represented the Sun. Our lives after marriage were the same as before, except we filed joint tax returns and going forward through life, there would always be four cats. It was almost our first anniversary, but on this day our world changed when Timmy suddenly cried out and emerged from behind the sofa slowly dragging his left hind leg.

"He needs the vet now," said Melissa.

There was no time for a cat carrier; she wrapped him in a towel and we ran downstairs. In the back of the cab, I saw tears and reached for Melissa's hand. The vet saw us right away but Melissa knew it was already too late. As she held him in the cab, I was unaware that his little soul had already ascended to heaven. A clot had wended its lethal way to his sweet heart and stopped it forever.

Melissa couldn't bring herself to say anything until we were alone in the examining room. Grief was a very private thing for Melissa; she needed no attention. All she wanted was to be alone with her cat and cry in private. I didn't know how to comfort her. I had only experienced death with Grandma and Ruth, and I was surprised at the impact the death of Timmy was having on me. Wiping tears, we took one last look and I bundled Melissa back into a cab. Back at the apartment, we were greeted by Robin, Onion, and Sammy, who somehow knew. The sadness in the air could be cut with a knife. Even though Timmy had a one-digit IQ, his absence left a hole in our apartment and our hearts.

Two months later, Melissa bounded in the door holding in her arms a year-old white cat with random black spots, wistful blue eyes, and a stocky muzzle.

"What the hell is that?"

"Hi, Honey. Isn't he cute? The vet asked if I wanted him—for free! Someone found little Oscar who either ran away or was abandoned. The vet tried to find his original owners but it's been almost six months. Oscar needs a good home and the vet thought of us."

"Why do we have to have four cats?"

"The vet said Oscar was confused and depressed about living away from his original family so he needs some fattening up and lots of love and attention," said Melissa, willfully ignoring my questions.

Don't we all, I thought and recalled my hurt when my family forgot about me before my brother's wedding. I had been symbolically abandoned. Oscar was literally abandoned and I'm not sure there's a difference but I was sure that my darling wife was playing me like a song. Watching Oscar greet his new brothers, my eyes went vacant wondering if I would have missed my family.

It would take more than a year for Oscar to become attached to us. We patiently waited as Oscar grew into a sturdy, handsome cat that would be our protector and cozy up when we were in pain or needed comfort. The sixth sense reigned true in cats. They seemed to know just what you were thinking, good or bad. Within days, Melissa sang to the tune of "Frosty the Snowman" as she held her new cat:

"Oscar the kitty,
Was as fine as he could be.
With a turned up tail and a button nose
And two eyes that look at me."

It warmed my heart to hear her sing knowing she was shedding the pain of Timmy, and receiving love from Oscar, a new band-aid. The beautiful white of Oscar's coat shed so much we could have made a Persian rug every day; there were chunks of white fur everywhere. You could never actually see the furniture after Oscar sat on it—just white fur mixed with some black from his spots. Speaking of flying carpets, Melissa and I had a long weekend scheduled at the Jersey Shore. On this trip, Melissa decided to fret over Oscar.

In the car, she looked at me and said, "I wonder what poor Oscar is doing? It is his first vet stay since we took him. Probably thinks we don't want him."

I took a deep breath. "He's a cat. He's fine in the kitty condo."

My hands were sweating on the wheel thinking of the dollars it cost to board four cats where they were taken out twice a day for exercise and huge flat screens entertained them 24/7 with pictures of butterflies, insects, and birds. We also paid the added fee for online viewing. And when we picked them up, they would be bathed, nails clipped and scented with perfume. We stopped for soda and I knew she was still upset, probably thinking about Timmy. I motioned with my fingers mimicking the antenna of an insect and said, "You're looking for trouble. You remind me of Mom, cleaning our house in the middle of our vacation."

"Great," said Melissa. "We're married for barely a year and you're already comparing me to your mother? I want a divorce!"

"You're such a loving Mommy leaving your cats in a den of anal probes, shots, and pills." She made a face. "Your precious Oscar will have to endure incarceration and a bath!"

That forced a smile and Melissa relaxed until the engine started smoking on, of all places, the Garden State Parkway, on a perfect beach day. Obviously, this day was shot.

"Stop!" said Melissa as smoke billowed from the hood.

"Okay, don't worry," I said, slowing down as flames shot from the engine. I swerved to a stop on the shoulder and Melissa darted out screaming for me to get out. For some reason, I moved in slow motion. I turned the engine off.

"Get out!" she yelled. "What is wrong with you?"

Death flashed through my mind, but didn't sway me. I knew it wasn't my time. I had no fear of the flames, in fact, peace settled over me knowing I was not afraid to die. I didn't want to die; I just had no fear of it. Maybe I *was* being a little passive aggressive and I did love making Melissa crazy. I was definitely angry that we still had four cats and that we would always have four cats no matter how many died. Maybe I just knew that life follows death just as death follows life and somehow the two were related. I got out of the car.

CHAPTER 24
PARIS FIRST, THEN THE BABY

Most marriages are followed by one or more additional souls entering into the world. It's the natural cycle of life; a child is a manifestation of the parents' love. As we considered getting pregnant, it felt right, but there was a nagging, small voice in the back of my head. Long ago, an astrologer told me that if I had children, I would derive very little joy from the experience. Thinking I had already paid my karmic dues, we proceeded on course and it felt right. We purposefully waited eighteen months before trying to conceive, something Melissa's mother threw in our faces on our latest visit.

We were in their living room when Evelyn asked me to go into the guest bedroom to get the baby blanket she knitted. Baby blanket? She was in a wheelchair wearing a smirk on her face. When I neglected to move, she blurted out,

"I can't hold my tongue any longer. I want a grandchild!"

Melissa turned three shades of red and driving home, we spoke at length about wanting a child. The streetlights blurred as we tried to stay upbeat about a stressful, emotional subject. I thought we needed a change of pace.

"Hey, how about we fly to France?" I asked.

"What?" said Melissa.

"Let's see the Eiffel Tower before we make a baby," I said and did not get an argument.

One month later, we boarded a jet bound for Paris. We were flying to Paris for ten days and would be staying with some ex-pat friends who had a guest room in their apartment, which was six blocks from the Eiffel Tower. Spring in Paris was idyllic. The trees were covered in newborn green, and the shops overflowed with asparagus, strawberries, baskets of fresh-cut flowers, and crusty baguettes. From our balcony, we posed with the Eiffel Tower in the background, using colored lens filters of yellow, green and blue. We toured Notre Dame, visited the Louvre every chance we had and sailed down the Seine. As we got off the boat, Melissa spotted a street vendor with posters of *La Chat Noire* and rushed to make her first purchase.

In a nearby café, I tried to understand the menu. The French must feed all the chicken breasts to the cats because I couldn't find it on any menu. Somehow the parts we normally eat weren't available, but the food was delicious, so *c'est la vie*. Our best meal was at Jules Verne, in the Eiffel Tower. Another memorable meal, though much simpler, was crepes and a couple of bottles fermented apple cider somewhere on the Left Bank. All was well until it was time to leave, and an inebriated Melissa almost fell over, not realizing just how high the alcohol content was in that delicious, seemingly innocent cider. We joked that while in France we gained about three pounds in ten days, but whenever we visited Mom for good old southern cooking, we usually gained ten pounds in one week. I imagine the famous Krispy Kream donuts had something to do with that. Also, the sauces in France, no matter how good, were no calorie competition for southern biscuits, gravy, and ham.

Within twenty four hours of landing in New York, Melissa marched to the local bookstore to find books on ovulation and making babies. Once people find out you're trying to have a baby, conception becomes a communal exercise. Advice, encouragement and, sometimes, too much personal information, descended from all directions. We received advice on the best positions, listened to remedies for low sperm counts (not a problem, by the way) and a myriad of other hurdles we had to jump through before I could knock up my old lady. What happened to just hitting the sheets? As far as I was concerned, it sure was fun trying to get pregnant, whatever the excuse. We just kept trying, window or no window.

After reading everything she could get her hands on, Melissa and I took a quick trip to Hilton Head, South Carolina and Savannah, Georgia. Keeping stress at bay was always the key in the baby making process, and we took full advantage. We decided to drive to Savannah, looking forward to sampling pralines and other southern treats. We arrived and explored several of the 39 town squares reminding me of past days of glory which were not necessarily enduring in the present. It was as if we were back in time, just like Versailles. There was a sign advertising a ghost tour that night. We admitted that the idea was tempting, but I had a hunch that tonight was going to be the night to conceive.

I looked at Melissa and said, "Let me weigh my options: raw sex all night or a ghost tour? Let me think …"

Our eyes met and a light connected between us. Somehow we knew tonight was ordained.

CHAPTER 25
A CHILD IS BORN

Back in New York, Melissa bought what seemed like hundreds of dollars' worth of pregnancy tests to make sure she had her bases covered. I woke up one morning and heard, "I can't believe I missed it."

"Are you kidding? You can't aim and pee on an expensive stick? I can't do this for you."

"Every time I try, Onion or Sammy starts rubbing my leg and I get distracted. It's like they know what I am doing and they are giving us their blessing."

"Or, they are trying to mess up the test because they don't want the competition," I countered, pulling a pillow over my head. I remembered all the times we were on the Garden State Parkway on the way to see her parents and Melissa was driving. Stopping at a toll, she threw a quarter at an automatic coin machine, the size of Texas, and missed it repeatedly. Horns blew from impatient drivers behind us. People were flipping us the bird and who knows what they were yelling. The toll attendant three booths over was also glaring at us. Melissa threw harder each time, still missing her mark. With one quarter left, I leaned over, made a two-point shot and we were on our way.

Now, I laughed thinking of Melissa trying take aim at a small stick. But really, how hard could it be?

"Dean, get in here!" Melissa's voice was urgent.

Running to the bathroom, I pushed open the door to see her sitting on the toilet, panties down around her ankles, mouth open and holding out a pink pee stick for me to see.

"We're pregnant!"

The news hit us like a shockwave. I picked up Melissa and twirled her around sending ripples far into our universal future. We were going to bring life into the world. We called Melissa's parents and were met with a "pass the potatoes" attitude. Next, we called Virginia and there was a little more cordiality but no one did cartwheels there either. Despite being in her late thirties Melissa would have an uneventful pregnancy earmarked by regular sonograms that showed our little boy's development.

As Melissa's pregnancy progressed, we panicked realizing there was no room for a crib in our apartment. The same apartment that many years ago seemed so big, allowing me to expand my life, was now too small. I could almost hear the cracking of an egg as new life was emerging and bringing me to an even bigger world. With trepidation, resignation, and a touch of anxiety, I acknowledged that it was time to leave this rabbit hole where a lot of magical things had happened.

Despite our impending move, Theo kept me on as building manager. This building had become a part of me, and leaving it was like the soul shedding its body for another one, or when a child outgrows their old clothes and requires new. Though where you live isn't as important as how you live and who you are with, the esoteric bull didn't quell my ambivalence as we slogged through a nor'easter looking for new digs. We found a two-bedroom in a high-rise on 27th Street and Second Avenue, near New York University Hospital, where Melissa would deliver. From here, we knew our next step would be out of Manhattan and on to the suburbs.

Knowing we wouldn't be in our new apartment long didn't decrease the drama from our new neighbors, the yuppie scum who lived next door who treated Melissa as if she didn't have a belly the size of Alaska. They appeared to take great delight in beating her to get a cab, refusing to hold the elevator doors, and, generally, being pigs. When another festive year came to an end, it was time to dispose of our Christmas tree and the garbage room was just past the yuppie doorway . . . so, I decided that revenge would be sweet. For some reason, as I passed their door, the dead tree accidentally, *on purpose*, slipped from my hands and deposited a nice two-inch heap of brown pine needles on their welcome mat. I was so proud. Looking back down the hall, I saw Melissa doubled over with laughter and I did it once more just for the hell of it.

One warm day in May, just two weeks shy of her due date, Melissa thought it would be a good idea to spend the morning laboring in the kitchen over lasagna. She energetically stirred the meat sauce and seasoned the ricotta filling. The critters peacefully looked on, not getting in Melissa's way. They seemed to know just how to take care of her. Even Sammy finally settled down after spending his first month at our new digs meowing all night long, announcing his displeasure to the world. No wonder our new neighbors hated us. I was salivating all day and couldn't wait to sit down to a delicious meal. I was called to the table, and a nice portion was placed in front of me accompanied by a red leaf lettuce salad. When Melissa went back into the kitchen to bring extra cheese, I sneaked a taste and nearly choked. It was bad, *really* bad. I don't know what she did; I don't want to know. It had the consistency of a brick and tasted like one. Pregnancy had definitely affected the quality of her cooking. Stealing a guilty glance at the kitchen doorway, I panicked; how was I going to tell her the meal she had spent all morning preparing could even gag someone who had no sense of taste or smell and should go in the garbage as hazardous waste?

"AHHHHHHHHHH!" Melissa screamed.

I ran to find her hunched over holding her stomach. A thousand things flashed through my mind: call a cab, call the doctor, did her water break? I'm still hungry. Where's a dinner I can actually eat? I can't handle things when I'm hungry, and, finally, I'm going to be a dad. I wrapped my arms around Melissa and walked her to the nearest chair. Gathering the already packed suitcase, I commenced the ritual performed by thousands of dads before and thousands yet to come. I was experiencing the full rite of passage from bachelor to husband to father, and now my only concern was for Melissa.

But before I hailed a cab I *did* remind her that her doctor said she should try to walk to the hospital. We caught a cab and rode to NYU where Melissa smiled through each contraction and did her Lamaze breathing without complaint. That's our story and I'm sticking to it. Settled in her room, I watched the fetal monitor next to her bed, coaching her and timing the contractions. When I saw the graph line dip, I gently informed her that the contraction was over.

"How the hell could you know when it's over? Fuck you," she screamed, sweating and panting. I immediately resolved to carefully gauge my facial expressions because I knew that every twitch, gesture or even a solemn poker face could be construed to mean something else and would be ingrained in Melissa's memory for all time. Every mother on earth can recall, with amazing clarity, chapter and verse whatever the father of her child did or said during her labor, and, at the most inopportune times (like when the dad is winning an argument).

I guess it's a small price to pay for the hours and hours Melissa labored to birth our son. I held her hand, talked, stayed quiet, wiped her brow, and watched the second hand on the clock where each minute seemed like an hour. At 5:00 a.m., the doctor came in and told us Melissa's labor was not progressing as he would like and that he recommended a "C" section. Panic ensued as our Lamaze instructor never got to that part. Blood rushed to my neck and face; our baby was preordained, meant to be, why didn't he just come out?

A blue screen was placed over Melissa's waist blocking our view of the operation. I saw the nurse hand the doctor the scalpel and had to sit down. Of course, Melissa was numb from the waist down and I was ordered not to look beyond the screen, just like the *veil* I'm not supposed to see. At 6:09 on a Monday morning, our world changed forever.

"It's a boy!" the doctor said, and I leaned over to kiss Melissa and push the hair back from her face.

"It's our boy," I whispered as she smiled.

Loud crying erupted amongst the shuffling that went on "down there" but I heard angel trumpets.

"Ten fingers and toes," said the doctor.

Melissa burst into tears and was shaking but I knew everything was right with the world.

As they swaddled the baby, we held hands and looked into each other's souls. Our son was handed to us, all seven pounds and three ounces, with strawberry blonde hair. Everything was perfect. Holding him for the first time, his eyes were open, beautiful blue eyes. He was so small, so needy. Without words, I told him I would be there for him, always. Melissa's green eyes shone with excitement and wonder.

"We have a baby," she said.

"He is all ours."

I thought of my grandmother and wished she was here to see my son, this new life that we had created. One precious soul had sprung from the fusion of two cells; a bursting mix of energy, life and love that was the beautiful boy I held in my arms. Where does new matter come from? It came from us: Melissa and me. And here is our boy, Craig, who will change the world.

Melissa fell asleep in the recovery room so I used the time to go home and freshen up. I returned home at about 11:00 a.m. and threw some dry cat food in a bowl. As usual, the four cats formed a welcoming committee, rubbing and circling around my ankles as I sat to make the calls.

"Evelyn, you have a grandson, Craig, and your daughter is fine. He was born at five this morning."

"Oh, thanks for calling. You know I have been up all night waiting for you to call. We'll drive up tomorrow or the day after."

"What jerks," I said when I hung up. She never missed a chance for drama while never realizing it only revealed her self-centeredness.

"Hi, Mom, you have a grandson, Craig. Melissa is doing great."

"I'm glad everything is okay. Do you want me to fly up when Craig comes home? I know Melissa will need help."

"We'll let you know, Mom. Melissa wants to get Craig settled in before we make any plans."

I slept on the couch till mid-afternoon, and according to the list near the phone, I must have called at least 15 people before I passed out, but I don't remember. When I awoke, I tried calling my favorite cousin, Ellen, again before going back to the hospital. I was surprised when her husband picked up. He sounded as if something was wrong.

"Tom, I was expecting Ellen. Why aren't you at work?"

"There's been ... How's Melissa? Did you guys have the baby?"

"Melissa gave birth this morning and everyone is great. We named him Craig and I wanted you and Ellen to know. May I speak to her?"

"Congratulations!" Tom said, but the word didn't hold a smile.

"What's wrong, Tom?"

"It's Ellen's dad. He died over the weekend and the funeral was today. The doctor said his heart just stopped and Ellen flew down to Atlanta yesterday. You know he and Ellen have been estranged for quite a while."

Onion knew there was trouble and jumped up on my lap, rubbing his muzzle on my leg as if to console me. "I'm so sorry. He was …" I paused because I knew Ellen had a rocky relationship with her father but had been good times, too.

"I'll miss him," I sad. "Please tell Ellen that and explain why I cannot come down."

My happiness and elation were now juxtaposed with pain and sadness. As I reached to pet Onion, I thought of the days ahead for Ellen, wishing I could be there for her. I was in such a tender, emotional place. One soul leaves the world, another enters. Death and labor were equally bitter and sweet, ascending to God and descending from Him. As I dressed, I listened to the radio and sang along to *All you Need is Love* by the Beatles not realizing how wise and prophetic those simple words would prove to be.

The next day at the hospital, Melissa was nursing Craig while I read the cards that accompanied the flowers sent by friends and family. Melissa's room looked more like a florist shop, or that serene arboretum in Hana, rather than a sterile hospital room. However, all too soon our peace was interrupted. To our horror, we recognized the shrill voices of Melissa's parents approaching like an unexpected storm. We actually heard them arguing, disrupting the quiet of the maternity ward, as Jim pushed Evelyn's wheelchair into Melissa's room. Melissa and I knew we would have to shield Craig from her parents and, possibly, from mine. They would not poison their grandson's life as they tried with their own children. We both cringed as James pushed Evelyn in her wheelchair into the room to greet their first and only grandchild. James placed a canned ham on Melissa's nightstand and told the world of his earth-shaking generosity. Evelyn handed me a ceramic vase, shaped like a bootie, and wasted no time pouting over all the other vases and baskets of flowers.

"I thought mine would be the only one."

My first instinct was to protect my son from this barrage of negative energy. Melissa's parents were like a swarm of gnats. You could swat at them all you wanted but they would just regroup, undeterred, and come at you again. I took Craig from Melissa who fixed herself the best that she could. Evelyn cooed and wanted to hold him. I placed Craig in her one good arm and supported his back. For a second, her eyes were radiant and I glimpsed the mother she could have been, but her strength soon gave out and I held Craig once more. Maybe that was it: Evelyn didn't have the strength to be a good mother. *Maybe.* The rest of Jim and Evelyn's visit revolved around their usual litany of complaints, self-pity, and bad news. Whenever it became unbearable, I thought of the cats using their suitcase as a litter pan and that got me through until we saw the back of them. Then it was just me, Melissa, and our beautiful baby boy, Craig. I was happy.

Three days later, we brought our boy home. At the head of our little parade, I carried Craig in his car seat, one of our wonderful doormen helped Melissa and several more followed with balloons and flowers. Once in our apartment, Melissa whispered,

"What was I thinking? I must have been crazy. Get your mom here now; I'm going to need help."

Before I called Mom, I helped an exhausted Melissa into bed. The cats were wild for Melissa but, instinctively, knew that they needed to be gentle. All four of them curled up in pile at the foot of our bed, not missing a thing as I tried to make her comfortable. Only Onion ventured close to Melissa and even then, he just lay by her side, a quiet and attentive presence. Besides, I knew the real excitement was the human kitten in my arms as I put a sleepy Craig in his bassinet. With two-thirds of my household sound asleep, I called Mom and made arrangements for my parents to fly to New York the next day. The first thing Mom did to *help* was prepare a big pot of beans for post-operative Melissa.

"Your mother hates me," said Melissa. "I was better off alone."

Observing Craig in his bassinet was like watching a Mexican jumping bean. He squirmed, grabbed each side of his bassinet and shook it. He also managed to turn himself over on his tummy at two weeks old. Of course, we both thought he was adorable but we suspected we had a wild man on our hands. Our little boy cried every three hours for his feedings and that was alright by me: it was what a baby does and what nature intended, though, I am sure, it was losing its allure for his Mommy. However, nature did not intend for me to forget to close the piano lid one night and have Sammy scare the hell out of us by walking on the keys at three in the morning. As I stumbled to the living room, Melissa helpfully inquired, "Why would an intruder play the piano?" Then we both heard Craig cry and it wasn't funny anymore. If there had been an axe next to the bed, Melissa would have used it.

The cats immediately bonded with Craig. Every afternoon at 4:00 p.m., they lined up and paraded into Craig's room, tails held high, for a nap in the warm late-day sun. Onion loved to lie on Melissa's baby pillow while she nursed Craig. When Craig got a bit older, Binky would lie down beside him and let him explore his fur with his chubby little hands. Amidst all this tender feline care, there was only one flagrant act of rebellion against our son. Some unknown feline (Sammy) peed in Craig's diaper bag but that was the only false note in the growing bond between Craig and the cats. There was something soothing in the rhythm of this routine during our transitional period. We were becoming a family.

All too soon, Craig was crawling and our apartment was happily crowded with baby toys. We purchased a portable baby swing which proved to be indispensable because it was the only way Craig could go to sleep and we sorely needed the relief. One Saturday evening, Melissa put a screaming Craig into the swing, turned on the machine, and nothing happened. She tried repeatedly and began to panic when we realized Craig was now too heavy for the batteries to power the swing. Melissa started to cry.

"I think it is time to move to the suburbs," I said. We both knew our goals in Manhatttan had been met. Craig was one-year-old and now it was time to move from the City and onward to Connecticut. We had no choice, at least within our price range. We needed more room and wanted a backyard, the typical excuses everyone gives, so we bade farewell to Manhattan. I had lived in the City for twenty years and Melissa for fifteen, but leaving Manhattan was like leaving Hawaii. Melissa held on tight to whatever she could find until I finally had to drag her out kicking and screaming.

We followed the movers up I-95, still not convinced we had made the right decision. Compounding our dismay was a two-hour traffic jam during which Onion pooped in his carrier which was crammed in front seat between Melissa and me. Once again, Sammy yowled at the top of his lungs without pause. Craig slept through it all but we knew that meant he would be up late. Four hours later, we arrived at our new home with a cathedral ceiling in the living room, a Jacuzzi in the master bath, and a huge kitchen with brand new appliances.

"It's too quiet!" griped Melissa our first morning as new home owners. "And when I finally dozed off, the birds woke me up at four o'clock in the morning."

"Listen, *Miss Bitch, Piss and Moan*," I said, not up for any verbal sparring with my beloved. "So you prefer the familiar sounds of New York City, huh? Let's take a walk down memory lane: sanitation workers collecting garbage at five in the morning, crazy people shooting porn movies on the roof of our apartment building, and, don't forget your personal favorite, all the times Craig's baby monitor picked up the conversations of Pakistani taxi drivers in the middle of the night."

No answer, just banging pots; Melissa's dissatisfaction was duly noted. She was in mourning. I was surprised Melissa didn't don widow's weeds, retire from society with stacks of *New York Magazine*, and weep. It took two years for Melissa to get the hang of her new fresh air life. Who would have ever guessed that one day she would wait impatiently for the seed catalogues to arrive? Or be able to converse intelligently on the merits of annuals versus perennials. *Not*

119

me. In time, she even learned not to freak out when the skunk, that loved to climb the lilac bush outside the master bedroom window would bless our house with his unforgettable nectar. We even kept a supply of tomato juice on hand, just in case.

Another bonus of suburban life was that the cats constantly wanted outside, then inside, then outside again. Since our boys were city cats, who had only experienced the outside world through the windows of apartment buildings, there was a brief but traumatic period of adjustment. However, the cats soon discovered that their new home was a kitty wonderland. Birds, bugs, squirrels, and chipmunks were plentiful, and any sighting required them to dash outside, and Melissa had a new career; she became an unpaid doorman.

Beginning a new life in this new dimension was good. Like shedding skin, we discarded our old habits and routines for new. Living once again where grass and trees were plentiful allowed me to feel the ground under my feet, rooted as I've never been before. Like Robin's purr expanding outward, I too sensed my energy field broadening. We learned terms like "Connecticut coif," the hairdo favored by every too-tan, tennis-playing matron on the Gold Coast. We also chafed against the not-so-subtle inbred caste system so common in the suburbs. In the city, we dined next to celebrities or grabbed a dog at Gray's Papaya; it didn't matter. Here, if you were not somebody, you were nobody. And we could no longer hold our noses up with our 212 area code. We were 203, like everyone else.

CHAPTER 26
DASH

The phrase, *The King is dead; long live the King*, in our household applied to our cats. Though I rescued Robin from the windowsill in Manhattan, this time I couldn't save him. Six months after our move to Connecticut, Melissa watched the Bink pitifully try to jump up on the sofa. The next day she observed him walking down the hall, his body noticeably rounder, and she knew something was terribly wrong. It wasn't long before we heard the vet say the word, "cancer". His body was growing larger as the cancer flowered unchecked and there was nothing we could do; he was 16 years old. Melissa was inconsolable but she had to keep her emotions in check because of Craig. It was Halloween when the vet placed the Bink on a cold metal table. There were strange animal smells everywhere mixed with the odor of disinfectant. I felt like I was in an airport, where nervous energy abounded, and all I wanted to do was bolt. Melissa and I watched as a small patch of fur was shaved from his leg. Melissa placed her head against Robin's as the first shot was administered.

"This is to relax Robin" said the vet. As she pressed the handle of the second shot, she said, "Now, this one will stop his heart. He won't feel anything. You did the right thing."

His body became limp as another dear soul passed to the other side. The remains on the table were simply discarded clothes but I put my ear on his chest and still heard gurgling within his dead body. I looked at Melissa as her body was wracked with sobs. No matter how many times you hear, "He lived a good, long life" it still doesn't erase the fact that his "good, long life" was now over. My stomach was unsettled as if I'd just eaten a dozen sour pickles. Needles pierced the back of my eyes as I tried to hold back tears.

We returned home, filled a bowl with candy and stuck it outside the front door. Craig was too young to know it was Halloween and we couldn't have cared less. Our darling Robin was gone. What a somber, miserable day this was and how would we ever explain to Craig that our beloved Binky was gone forever? I knew there was always balance in Nature and Melissa would ensure that the void would be quickly filled but we loved him and would miss him always.

The same night that Binky died, Melissa and I were in bed and it felt like the Angel of Death was hovering over us. It was a palpable feeling of warning. Melissa looked at me with fear in her eyes and I knew she felt it too. It could not possibly be from Binky who was such a wonderful soul. We both struggled to sleep and by morning the specter had lifted. I shrugged it off as being Halloween hype but the next afternoon while Melissa was making cupcakes for our church, the call came that Melissa's father had just suffered a massive stroke.

For the next three weeks, Melissa drove back and forth from Connecticut to New Jersey to tend to her parents, putting our family's life on hold. It was perfectly acceptable to Evelyn and Jim for Melissa to sacrifice her time with her family and wait on them. Melissa begged her parents to go into a continuing care facility or, at the very least, senior citizen housing. They could have easily afforded either but her father wouldn't hear of it. Evelyn, who required more medical care than Jim, was receptive to the idea but Jim chose to cling tenaciously to his home. He insisted that Melissa hire home aides who, along with all their incumbent drama, would rob them blind, including writing a check to one of their accomplices for $25,000.

Eventually, life settled back to normal, and a month later, Melissa and Craig walked in the front door and Melissa called with excitement, "Dean, come and meet Dash." In her arms was another furry investment of time and money in which I had absolutely no say in its acquisition.

"Dash is a very special kitty; he had to be rewired with female plumbing because of chronic urinary problems. The owners refused to pay the bill so we got him for free."

"Free," I thought to myself, was a grossly inexact term because I knew full well sticker shock would catch up with us sooner or later. So we were now the proud owners of a transsexual cat and just like Oscar, this so-called *free* cat came complete with a one year "no charge" health guarantee. I wondered if my wife was listed on a website devoted solely to crazy cat people with a savior complex. Dash, Melissa's ninth cat and my sixth, had big yellow eyes and a medium build. His fur was mostly white with black patches in the most peculiar places that inspired one of our neighbors to christen him "Cow Cat" because his fur made him look just like a miniature Holstein. Initially, we all wondered why he was given the name "Dash" but when I opened the front door, we found out. Dash did, indeed, dash out the door, presenting Melissa even more opportunities to open and close the door repeatedly throughout the day.

Dash loved the outdoors and would usually leave the house around May and not return, except for meals, until late October. I would come home from work and observe Dash, along with the other cats, *living heaven on earth* as they stared into a raised clump of grass in our neighbor's front yard that was an irresistible treasure trove of those small tasty chipmunks.

"Hey, Melissa, I have a new name for our neighbors' patch of fancy grass. Let's call it the *Grassy Knoll*."

"That's not all," said Melissa, clearly in an "I can top that" mood. "Yesterday, I was taking out the garbage and noticed Dash, Oscar and that big butt, Marmalade from up the block (rumored to have killed squirrels) gathered by my car. I never saw a more guilty looking collection of cats. It felt like I was intruding on a secret meeting. This morning I took Craig out to his swing set and it was just disgusting. Pieces of small rodents were scattered all over our backyard. I tried to kick one away from Craig's swing and its intestines unfurled all over the ground. Gross."

I sighed; not so long ago we led much different lives. Now, we converse about grassy knolls, an orange tabby that may or may not have killed squirrels, and intestines spiraling out of a dead mouse. I watched my life pass each day as I looked through commuter train windows. Trees, houses, and buildings passed by in a blur as I filled three hours a day getting back and forth to work. While I worked my tail off passing paper back and forth, creating and answering emails, our cats stayed home, lounged around all day and enjoyed *their house.* I just slept there, as Melissa always kindly reminded me; she did the actual living. I came to the conclusion that I must be doing penance for something horrible I did in a past life. Since I first met Melissa, my goal in this life has never wavered; I want to be re-incarnated as one of Melissa's cats.

Cats personify the word "sinecure," meaning they hold high positions of authority and do absolutely nothing. Our cats had everything they needed: cat beds, which they dismissed for our bed, fresh people food whenever they wanted, a toddler to play with, and enough cat and boy toys to keep them occupied for years. Outside, they had birds, chipmunks and squirrels to chase and catch at will, not to mention watching their humans run constantly on our proverbial hamster wheels of life which, I have no doubt, entertained them the most. The care and love we gave these animals was far greater than any we had ever received from our families; so, why did we do it? These cats showed us something profound. The *veil* was close, ready to break at the seams, but first my eyes needed to prepare for the intense light that was to come. We didn't know it yet but our lives were about to change.

CHAPTER 27
HOUSTON, WE HAVE A PROBLEM

Some people would look up at the night sky and see beautiful stars reminding them of God and His glory, while others predicted rain or saw portents of disaster. From a distance, our lives looked perfect but, on closer examination, all was not as it seemed. Melissa and I, conscious of what we had experienced as children, did not want to repeat it with our son. We would always remember our pasts through a looking glass, fully aware that our parents knew better, and intent that we would do better for Craig.

Regardless of the astrologer's warning, I knew from an early age that if I had children, I would derive very little pleasure compared to the burden of responsibility which would ensue. "You were born under Leo," the astrologer explained, "and you came close to death at your birth." I knew this was true. "Pluto's force, if survived, will make you powerful later in life, with difficult karma to work through," he continued. "At the end, you will have wealth you do not have to work for, similar to unconditional love that is not earned." He also told me that real estate would consume a significant amount of my life (at the time I was already managing Theo's buildings). The final thing he said perplexed me, "You're an old soul with a young chart and your life will be painful but you are here for a reason. Others will not see you for who you are until later in life. With a moon in Scorpio, you have a tainted mother and your path will always be difficult. It is your nature."

Before Craig, life was good; the burdens of my karma were far from my mind. Melissa and I made good incomes, saw every Broadway play, and thought nothing of going out to outrageously expensive restaurants or taking extravagant vacations. I foolishly believed my destiny had changed, and that I was granted a reprieve from my fate. Eighteen months after Craig was born, I stood in my driveway, ankle deep in six inches of snow. A thin glaze of ice crystals mirrored the stars in their ancient configurations against the endless obsidian of night when, suddenly, a shard of light broke my reverie as it arced across sky, a beautiful herald of impending doom.

By spring, as if on cue, Melissa and I noticed changes in Craig. Our loving, responsive son no longer looked us in the eye. He stomped and threw things, indifferent to our pleas or attempts at discipline. Whenever we hugged him, Craig struggled out of our grasp as we strained for a glimpse of the child we had known. No matter what we did or said, we couldn't reach him. We continued to flail along, picking up the pieces of Craig's increasingly difficult behavior.

Soon it became difficult to take Craig anywhere. He was kicked out of Sunday school and banned from Gymboree due to his outbursts and quirks. The first time we took Craig to a barber we sat him in the raised chair and turned on a Smurf cartoon on the television in front of him. Melissa and I were happy because this was our son's first haircut—a momentous occasion. The barber made his first cut and Craig pulled off his red striped bib and screamed at the top of his lungs as if someone had cut off his fingers, one by one. The barber stopped, put the bib away, turned off the movie, and demanded that we leave. The second time, we were prepared but it took three adults to hold Craig down while he got his much needed haircut. As a parent, I may as well have consented to major surgery without anesthesia. Another time, in the men's room at the mall, I was at the urinal when Craig ran out. It was impossible to stop right away and my worst fears surfaced: he'll be abducted, he'll get lost, he won't know how to find me or where to go. When I rushed out, he was crouched in the middle of the walkway holding his ears. Only then did we realize that he was hypersensitive to sound; the hand dryers may as well have been torture devices.

Desperate, I called Theo who said, "Imagine being turned around in circles for five minutes and suddenly stopped. Disorientation and dizziness is the world Craig lives in. Nothing works for him. At an early age, he found himself caught in world where he does not fit in. He is angry and can't handle the frustration. In time, he may be able to learn to adapt."

The angry, judgmental looks we received in public brought me back to Tidewater all over again. Glares from the neighbors terrorized us, as one by one, Craig was no longer welcome to play with their children. Whenever she needed to leave the house, Melissa made sure other children weren't playing outside, to spare Craig. She was held hostage by all around her, and it was taking a toll. Even the women in our church's mothers' group treated Melissa like a leper; no one wanted anything to do with us. Suddenly our expanding universe began to reverse and collapse upon itself, returning to the original state of singularity. Craig was withdrawing from the world; our child was shutting down. Desperate for answers, Melissa spent countless hours with our pediatrician who dismissed our concerns.

"He'll grow out of it," she said, even though Melissa laid out her concerns in no uncertain terms.

"I know I'm an older mother," said Melissa, "and I don't have the energy of a twenty-five year old. I'm overweight and have little experience raising kids but I'm telling you this is too hard. Something is wrong."

"He's a boy and hyperactive," said the doctor. "Come back when he's three; then the State can evaluate your child."

Getting nowhere with the pediatrician, we sought out child psychologists. In one waiting room where the children were playing with battered toys and Melissa filled out another endless batch of forms, the doctor reprimanded me for Craig's behavior in the waiting area.

"Why the hell do you think we're here?" I said.

"Based on what I see, your son is not the type of child we treat."

"Then where do we go?"

No answer. We left the charlatan's office and were back in no man's land without a compass. Another psychologist told us, "Craig has a very bad case of ADD, the worst I've ever seen." Unfortunately, this doctor didn't know what do to, either. We heard this over and over: you have a problem but I don't know how to fix it. Sorry.

Our love and unyielding devotion to our son served as our only navigation tools. We despaired that they weren't enough but we never gave up. At this time, the world was not prepared for our son. Craig's attention span was a nanosecond, except when he was on the computer or when Melissa was reading to him. I told Theo about this, thinking we had made a breakthrough, only to learn that this was called "perseveration," when a child focused on one thought or idea to the exclusion of all else. Though we were discouraged, the computer provided a necessary oasis in our house. It provided a much-needed reprieve from his running, jumping, and constant need for supervision.

Sometimes, the only way to sooth Craig was to put him in our car and drive aimlessly for hours. The hum of the engine and the constant change of scenery calmed him down. He would exclaim, "A light show!" as twilight fell and red brake lights would contrast with yellow street lights and the bright, multicolored neon strip mall signs. For Craig, this was Disneyland, perhaps, as close as he would ever get. My heart throbbed with a pain so raw, no medicine could cure it. Back in our living room, I watched Craig stomp back and forth from room to room, up and down the stairs.

"The mass of the Earth is much denser than that of Venus," said Craig. I told Melissa the computer was doing him good; this was an accurate and intelligent thing to say, but another call to Theo dashed my hopes again when he correctly identified Craig's behavior as "scripting."

"Craig can't process what he hears, making it difficult to formulate his thoughts in words. He repeats things from television shows or computer games in an effort to communicate."

Another day, Melissa called me at work and told me she left the living room to go to the bathroom, and, when she returned, she found that Craig had climbed on the dining room table and was swinging from the chandelier. The cats were dismissed from our thoughts and our parents were forgotten; we concentrated only on Craig. At Theo's urging, we went to New York to consult a children's shrink and hired the sister of our usual babysitter to watch Craig.

Upon returning, I asked, "How did it go?"

No answer.

"Have I offended you in some way? Are you all right?"

"I'll never have kids! I'll never come here again!" she screamed.

"Welcome to my world!" yelled Melissa as she slammed the door.

But, at last, there was light at the end of a very long tunnel. Craig was three and enrolled in the church's preschool program, and it didn't take long before the telephone rang. At first, Craig's day was shortened in the hope that it would be easier for him. It wasn't. Next, the amount of days he attended preschool were cut and eventually pared down to only one hour, once a week. It was clear to us that Craig's teacher thought we were unfit parents, possibly violent parents, of an unruly child, and she wanted him out. The teacher acted like we abused Craig and refused to even make eye contact with Melissa. There was no escape from the judgment of so-called professionals, irate strangers in supermarket lines, or Craig's grandparents.

"Your child is bad because you waited too long to have him," said Evelyn.

Even Theo expressed his doubts. "I think you have spoiled him. It's obvious but he'll grow out of it." We were surrounded by people who blamed us as we watched our world crumble.

By late October, the wheels were finally put into motion; Craig was to be formally evaluated by the State. The pediatrician agreed and so did the school. The day of Craig's in-class evaluation, I watched as Melissa pulled out a can of caffeinated Coke and poured it in a cup for Craig to drink. I thought, how did it come to this? But, I understood her reasoning. Melissa needed to guarantee that Craig would show the examiners what we always saw. A month later, the school psychologist informed us that our son had autism, specifically PDD/NOS, Pervasive Development Disorder Not Otherwise Specified. She paused for a moment, raising her eyebrows as Melissa and I stared at her with mouths agape. Up until then, our greatest fear had been a diagnosis of ADD.

"Now, you can object to our findings and request another test but, if you do, the State's services may be delayed or possibly cut."

I wanted to pull out a sword and cut her dragon throat and watch the unfeeling black blood ooze from her neck. Instead, I whispered to Melissa, "not otherwise specified" means "no damn clue."

If the experts had no clue, what were we supposed to do now? As the earth shifted below our feet, the magnetic polls reversed as my family sailed into the uncharted waters of physical therapy, occupational therapy, speech therapy, sensory integration, EEG's, and vision therapy in a boat with no rudder. Melissa and I couldn't look at each other, fearing our heartbreak, like quicksand, would swallow us whole. We collected Craig and walked to the parking lot like automatons. I buckled a squirming Craig in the car seat, turned on the ignition, and began the journey that would encompass the rest of our lives. We returned home exhausted. Melissa watched a video with Craig while I climbed the stairs, like a zombie, to our bedroom where I fell face down on the bed and didn't seem to stop falling.

I fell asleep on a rumpled pillow wet with tears. In the netherworld of dreams, I became a lion prowling along a gravel path at night. Unusual moonlight patterns danced on the rocks but I gently crushed them under my paws. A small, deformed zebra appeared, and I maneuvered unseen into the scrub and waited for the right moment to pounce. The zebra moved toward me, unaware of any danger. The muscles in my hind legs tensed as I sprang in the air. In seconds, my teeth were in its neck and the good, familiar taste of blood gushed in my mouth. The zebra trembled under my rage and I knew the kill would only temporarily ease my pain and hunger. In victory, I raised my head, my mane standing out in pride. My vision was honed and sharpened in the night. Like looking through an infrared lens, I saw what lurked in the underworld for the first time. The full Moon was high above. I raised my eyes but it was not the Moon; it was the Earth. I was dead looking at the Earth, where blues and yellows bring sunshine, and I was stranded here on the lifeless Moon.

Heart beating faster, I stood on all fours, strong and sure, and knew that I was conscious, still alive here on the other side. Death, like change, was not to be feared. I relaxed my muscles, lay down and licked my paws knowing that I could live in either world, in the pain of the Earth, or in the dead of the Moon, and survive. It was late afternoon when I awoke with the same tears in my eyes. Groggy, I focused on the pale blue curtains that unfurled and billowed as the heat came on in our bedroom. I remembered my grandmother and a dream of a *veil* separating heaven and earth. I longed for her guidance as fresh tears fell. I needed a guide, a beacon that would reveal my strength, to help me see whom I really was and who I had to be in this world to help my son. Dozing off again, I was comforted by this guidance, this message that I was not alone. I was now able to fall into a deep, nourishing sleep.

The next week, Melissa and I attended a support meeting just for parents of newly diagnosed children. I arrived straight from work and didn't know what to expect as I hurried into the institutional cinderblock building. I joined Melissa and looked around the room at the twenty or so people gathered around the large conference table. As each parent introduced themselves, I discovered that we were lawyers, construction workers, school teachers, doctors, and housewives. Some had lived their entire lives in Connecticut; others were transplants like us, and a few parents were born in Europe, South America or the Middle East. Most were birth parents but there was one couple who had adopted a girl and another who had adopted two brothers, both of whom had been recently diagnosed. What bound all of us together was the absolute devastation of autism; it was the common denominator that cut through all social and economic barriers.

"This is the most humbling experience life can bring," said the counselor. "Think of yourself as a traveler who has dreamt all his or her life to go to Paris. You learned to speak French, learned to cook French cuisine, and even studied maps of Paris so you would know the city as well as any native. You board the plane and are so excited; your dream is finally coming true, but something goes wrong and the plane lands in Amsterdam, instead. Everything you ever learned, prepared for, worked for, and hoped for is out the window. Your dream is quashed and your world has changed forever. We are here to help you re-orient and find your way."

As the session progressed, we learned about the mountains we would have to climb and the magnitude of the situation weighed me down. I couldn't be one of *these people*. My child wasn't one of *them*. There had to be another answer. Maybe Theo was right; Craig would grow out of "it" and we were wasting our time. Silently, I raged against the truth, pitying those around me whose children were truly afflicted, but, no, not my boy. With a single stroke of my clenched fist, I could have cleaved the table in half.

When the class ended, Melissa barely reached her car before she broke down and I wrapped my arm around her shoulder. As I watched her drive away, a tension rose up in my jaw and I bit down hard, almost grinding my teeth to dust. I sat slumped in my car staring at the dim yellow glow of a distant street lamp, not bothering to start the engine or notice the damp chill of a November night. A burst of the deepest emotional release I have ever experienced gushed forth. I was back teetering on the edge of that old, forgotten well, and this time I fell, completely engulfed by darkness. Crumbling over the steering wheel, I was limp, desolate, knowing there was no way out.

Gathering my wits and wiping my face, I fumbled to turn the ignition. As I checked my rearview mirror, I saw a path of gravel, its uneven, rough gray hues illuminated by the yellow glow of an old streetlight. I thought of the lion's paws walking with confidence over the gravel. Looking again at the streetlight, it became a beacon. Its yellow light was the sun, bringing life where there was none. I breathed in the misty air and oxygen flowed in my blood again, knowing I had been given a sign, a gift to show that I could handle all that lay ahead. That guidance and strength would prevail.

The next day, I phoned Theo to discuss the diagnosis. He asked to see the paperwork from the State, doctors and psychologists. Being a psychologist himself, he apologized for questioning our parenting skills. He explained that he was hoping beyond hope that it was just a phase, or us, and not autism because he knew the path we now had before us. Theo referred us to a chemist in the Chicago area who compounded vitamins and minerals for children like Craig. It was not traditional medicine but rather a re-alignment of the chemical compounds in the body to bring them all to a normal level. He believed so strongly in this type of therapy that he generously paid for our trip. We had to wait over six months for an appointment.

Theo was an extraordinary man. Not every landlord would laugh when his building manager informed him that a cat had urinated on his checkbook or destroyed rent checks worth thousands of dollars. I thought back to the magic of Theo's building that I still managed and the fact that I would have never met Ruth, Theo, or even Melissa if I had not moved there. My guardian angel had been very busy. It was strange how I had to get to the very edge of life in order to realize its value.

In late January, Craig was enrolled in a special education preschool. I took the day off from work, and Melissa and I pulled up to the new school. The first thing we saw was a very angry looking woman taking her son, strapped to a wheelchair, out of her minivan. Anger was what I saw but no one knew what she was really feeling. The child's blond hair was sticking out from under a navy blue protective helmet and he was wearing a weighted vest. Clearly, his body was very fragile. Occasionally, the boy smiled but, all too soon, his smile faded and he retreated deep within. This child was confined by his body as well as his mind. He had obviously already broken many bones in his body and all of this armor was to protect him from further injury. The weighted vest was also there to give him some sense of where his body was in space. We saw there were people who had worse problems that we did and vowed not to judge them as we had been judged.

Craig had a rocky start in this new school but Melissa and I thought he was making some progress. By April, his teacher requested a conference. There, she dropped the bomb that they were losing Craig and we should seriously consider medication. We were strongly against medication in such a young child but we also realized Craig needed to be calm in order for the therapies to gain a foothold. To Melissa, it was ridiculous to medicate a child as young as Craig so she put off the appointment as long as she could but, eventually, we found ourselves in a psychiatrist's waiting room.

We met another family whose son had a diagnosis similar to Craig's but he had a twitch near his right eye. Alarmed, Melissa started a conversation with the child's mother,

"How long have you been coming here?"

"This is our second year," she said. "You see this twitch? It is *Tardive Dyskinesia* caused by his medication and will not go away. We're here to see if there is anything the doctor can do to fix it."

"Oh my God," said Melissa. "I would think they would do better than put us at such risk."

"It's been a nightmare," said the mother before going in to see the doctor.

We were such virgins. A parent can choose, or not, to medicate their child, but that decision always comes with a price and to play medication roulette was a dicey prospect. Despite our reservations, Craig swallowed his first dose of Ritalin on his fourth birthday. Even though Craig could barely tolerate small doses of Ritalin, which made him even more hyperactive as the dosage wore off, it still helped him focus for a few hours every day so the therapists could help him. Through all these trials and tribulations, we knew deep inside we were on the right track, but, like a hamster wheel, the goal is never really obtained.

I thought of God and hoped for what I didn't really know. Melissa and I would always strive to take our boy back from the hold of autism, but anguish was rising within me, unabated, and taking hold. I was at the end of my rope. I would always be there for Craig but knew that he could never be there for me. Without love throughout my childhood, and finding a soul mate who also grew up in a loveless home, we now had a son who couldn't love us back. Closing my eyes, I tried to overcome the self-pity that threatened to overpower my reason and my love. I looked for the answer, the *veil* hidden behind my eyelids, the shades of bluish grey that wave in shadows without form. I prayed.

We pulled into the driveway and there was Dash, as always, patiently waiting for chipmunks by the grassy knoll. When Dash first entered our home, he ran into every room, giving each the once over and a cursory sniff, only to return to Craig's room where he jumped on his changing table and settled down for a nap. That's when Dash had claimed Craig as his own. It reminded me of when Binky slept on Melissa's head whenever she was worried or upset. Dash knew Craig needed a friend and, like any pet, Dash provided non-verbal companionship.

At dinner, Melissa prepared a family favorite, her delicious marinara sauce with mushrooms and garlic. As I made the salad and garlic bread, a ray of sunshine came through the kitchen window at the perfect angle and lit up the wall behind Craig. I heard a purr and saw Dash walking in silence and grace toward Craig. Dash jumped next to Craig and rubbed his head on Craig's little arm. Then, before my eyes, a miracle happened.

Craig responded; he reached out with his sauce-covered hand and touched Dash's white fur, then looked at me and smiled. At dinner, we watched Craig feed Dash spaghetti; marinara sauce was all over Craig's face, the chair, and the cat but we weren't bothered. Melissa and I stayed quiet and still; we didn't want to break the spell. Craig continued to look at Dash and pet him, relating to him in a way I hadn't seen in years. The blue grey pounded in my head, becoming brighter and brighter as a fissure broke open before my eyes and light poured in without sound or condition, other than an open heart, willing to receive. The warmth pierced my head and cascaded to my heart. Pain turned to joy as meaning and purpose filled my soul.

Dash planted his blue eyes on mine; he blinked but didn't turn away. I looked closer and saw inside Dash all the way to his soul. Dash granted me a glimpse of his purpose: to guide Craig, who would be his student for years to come. New clarity and purpose changed my life in the twinkling of an eye. I was again grounded on earth, knowing my journey, knowing I was not alone. Though I continued to swim in the pain and currents of everyday life, now I was ever watchful for small miracles.

And now Dash was the miracle. He was there for Craig when neighborhood kids slammed the door in his face or when the phone didn't ring when a schoolmate was having a party. Dash was there when Craig was the only one who came home from school on Valentine's Day without a card. Dash was there when neighborhood kids and parents ran by our sidewalk on their way to play dates, hoping we wouldn't see them. Dash would always be there for Craig to console him for living in a world where he seemingly did not belong.

Guardian angels had been dispatched and they were the cats. My past pain and heartache were revealed and illuminated through the interconnection of the *veil* and my soul, and the bridge between them were the cats. Through great despair, the mystery of these animals comforted me and I realized the middle claw wasn't so bad after all.

CHAPTER 28
BETTER TO STAY IN THE CAGE

Several weeks after our trip to Chicago to see the chemist, a package arrived filled with mineral and vitamin compounds designed exclusively for Craig. I looked at the package, jaded but hopeful. Opening the box, I found the invoice and almost fainted. Vet bills were one thing, but now I knew I would never be able to retire. We loved Craig and would always find a way to make this work. To our surprise and delight, the compounds combined with Craig's regular medication produced a noticeable difference in his behavior. He became more related and in a better mood. He would even occasionally make eye contact. We felt we could almost go out in public without making a scene.

At this stage of Craig's development, finding a babysitter was impossible. Melissa's parents couldn't help and mine preferred to stay in Virginia so we handled our family by ourselves. Many neighbors walked past our house with imaginary blinders on, not daring to look in our direction lest we were outside or near a window. On the rare occasions they did see me, I would see a fake smile and hear a muted "hello." They never stopped to talk; we all knew the drill. During one of our phone calls, Theo said, "His condition is likely to be harder on you and Melissa because the parents know what their child is missing, whereas Craig has no idea and probably does not care."

Although our situation was improving, I knew Melissa bore the brunt and all the signs of battle fatigue were clearly evident. When I offered to take Craig so she could get away, she would often say that sometimes it's better just to stay in the cage. For Melissa, leaving home sporadically for only an hour or so was too frustrating because all she could think about was when she had to return. All typical avenues of company and socialization with other mothers were usually unsuccessful because when a child becomes labeled, so does their mother.

I knew the stress was plucking away at Melissa when she shared with me her fantasy of calling a babysitter, emptying the bank account, getting in her car and driving west without looking back. Living full time with Craig was not easy. Melissa grew hypersensitive to all perceived criticism of her child. She had trouble sleeping and her auburn hair was now flecked with silver. Even a trip to the *Golden Arches* wasn't a relief. We usually ate in the car because Craig's behavior was still so unpredictable, especially if there was a play area. There was no way we would chance an incident where someone could react to Craig's behavior. After all, their child wasn't like ours; they were better parents.

So Melissa remained ensconced at home with Craig and the cats while, in her mind, I was commuting to a glamorous job at a plush office with a buxom assistant greeting me every morning with a latte. Forget that I commuted three hours a day on dirty trains, cramped together with other poor sods, on my way to a job that barely made ends meet. *And* I was usually greeted with grief instead of a latte. I knew neither of us had it very easy.

CHAPTER 29
WHAT FRESH HELL IS THIS?

The planets must have been aligned improperly. Melissa's mother was in the hospital with congestive heart failure while Sammy, being vulnerable from his feral beginnings, was dying of liver disease. It was almost too much to bear dealing with autism, congestive heart failure, *and* a dying cat. To make matters worse, our dryer had given up the ghost and we were putting our home up for sale so I could accept a better job in New Jersey.

"Can we put any more shit on this plate?" said Melissa bitterly as I drove up to the vet's office. It was three months since the diagnosis and, short of a transplant, we had tried everything. I fought back tears as I watched my furry soul mate fade away as Melissa walked toward the office door. I stayed in the car with Craig to spare him the agony. Sammy was only six years old, much too young to die. Because he was feral, something was probably lurking within from the very beginning but his small passing was a great burden to bear.

And today was my birthday. I quickly wiped away my tears; I didn't want Craig to see how upset I was now that we had to put my favorite cat to sleep. It certainly started off my special day with a bang. The next treat would be to drive to New Jersey where my mother-in-law lay dying in a hospital bed. Coming out of the vet's office, Melissa carried an empty, tattered carrier which I unceremoniously threw in the trunk. Her cheeks were wet as she kept her head turned away so Craig wouldn't see. For the next two hours, we played a Sugar Beats CD, ad nauseam, for Craig and drove to New Jersey in silence. We were hoping that Craig didn't understand.

Around lunch time, we walked into the ICU waiting room and Jim grunted "hello." Melissa's aunt and uncle were already there and took charge of Craig as we left to visit Evelyn. Evelyn was flat on the bed with a breathing tube stuck down her throat. Melissa blanched and I began to sweat. Evelyn flitted in and out of consciousness; the only sign of life was one squeeze for "yes," and two for "no." Melissa's uncle called a funeral home just to be prepared. My cell phone rang and it was a call from our realtor. She had some inane question which I quickly answered and hung up. The events of the day blurred in and out as I was in a fog, focusing only on what I must to get by.

After listening to her heart and checking vital signs, the doctor pronounced that Melissa's mother was stabilizing. Jim left and, after another hour, we decided to drive back home. It was dark by the time we reached Connecticut, but before we sought refuge in our sanctuary, our home, I pulled up to Dairy Queen. Craig certainly deserved something after this long day when he behaved like a perfect child and Melissa's relatives wondered what she was always complaining about. A small, soft-serve cone dipped in cherry topping was my birthday treat to myself. I knew Melissa had presents at home and they would be opened soon, but not tonight. I understood and licked the cone as I steered with one hand.

♣

Frantic to sell our house, we painted, cleaned out the clutter, and staged. It was our first experience selling a house, and it was nerve wracking having the general public scrutinize your home and your taste. Every Sunday, there was an open house so Melissa, Craig and I would go out for brunch, which meant another fast food joint where we ate in the car. Brunch was followed by a long drive to nowhere or maybe a visit to a playground at an off hour where we hoped no one would be around.

Two weeks after the house went on the market, we returned home thrilled to find twenty people still looking at our house. Our real estate agent, coifed and outfitted in the indigenous Connecticut style, had set up lovely refreshments graciously welcoming all the potential buyers. What a rush; we were finally going to dump this place and move on. Then my hopes were dashed when a boy screamed, "Look Mommy, they have mice!" The boy's proclamation was no different than having lightning strike the "For Sale" sign in the front yard. Our poor agent was wringing her hands, running after the potential commissions crying, "But that's impossible, they have four cats!" Within seconds, the house cleared out and our fuming agent left grumbling, blaming us, of course. Upon careful examination the so-called "mouse" was a chipmunk that had wandered in because the front door had been left open. Melissa found it behind a table and we tried to coax it out of the house but, instead, it found refuge under the sofa. The cats clawed and meowed but none were able to grab it. The next day, Melissa found the poor thing dead, probably from fright.

The next Sunday, a young, newly married couple walked in and fell in love with our home. I saw the new bride on our deck with an expression on her face as if she had just won the lottery. Her face, filled with hope and happiness, gave my heart a lift. I was proud that our home made her happy but her mother-in-law had a different view. Melissa and I were standing next to her when the old hag shouted from the next room,

"I'll give you ten thousand dollars on the spot if you don't buy this house."

"Cow," I said to myself as my heart sank but my despair was short-lived because later that evening we received the couple's offer and, after some minor quibbling, everything was settled. Hanging up the phone I said, "I guess we aren't the only ones on the planet with deranged parents."

So fate and initiative gave us the green light to move to the Garden State. Connecticut had hardly been a joy ride so it was time for new life lessons to hit us again with both barrels. Perhaps the Garden State would be fertile soil for the growth of our souls.

Now we were the potential home buyers, mercilessly sizing up homeowners, their taste, and lifestyle. Driving through New Jersey neighborhoods, we saw many options: beautifully crafted brick colonials, Tudors, and the Georgian architecture of my home state, which made sense since New Jersey was one of the original thirteen colonies.

"Quick! Start looking for the 'George Washington Slept Here' signs," I said. As soon as the words came out of my mouth, we saw the sign for the George Washington Headquarters Museum.

Our realtor drove up to a beautiful center hall colonial that sported a copper weather vane in the shape of a cat. A sign, I thought as a brisk wind spun the cat one way, then the other. Walking into the foyer with a beautiful marble floor, we saw the living room had two knockout stained glass windows. The kitchen was large but needed renovation, and, just like the Meyers' property, the landscaping was overgrown and woody. The house was a little over our budget but I knew I was a goner. Melissa had the same look on her face that the young bride did when she stood in our living room. We communicated without words and knew we were going to buy it. Cosmically speaking, this house had our name on it. That evening, the sellers accepted our bid even though ours was a little lower than another one they had received earlier in the day. Later, we learned that the lady of the house wanted us to have it because she felt a connection to Craig. We learned from our mistakes in Connecticut and purchased a home with a very private backyard, allowing Craig to play without noticing others were playing without him.

New Jersey had one of the highest rates of autism in the country, and, as a result, we received very good services. I wondered at the sudden increase in numbers of autism cases and I was constantly asking "why?" I knew the names of some of the culprits that had been bandied about for years: the preservatives found in the MMR vaccine, a genetic predisposition, environmental pollution, and the growing number of women giving birth later in life. But maybe the kids were being born to flourish in a technical world? We've just entered the information age, also known as the Age of Aquarius, defined by the phrase, "I know." Humanity was changing in not so subtle ways.

As we went to bed, all four cats performed their nightly ritual of jumping up and taking their respective positions. Thus, one daily cycle was coming to a close and we were about to process all our lessons in a REM sleep allowing us to awake to a new morning and start the cycle once again ... and again ... and again. This ritual of *Earth School* taught us to live one day at a time, moment by moment.

CHAPTER **30**
THE GARDEN STATE WITH REPROBATES

Cats, cats and more cats was my mantra as we moved to the Garden State, the eggplant capital of the world, fifth wealthiest state per capita in the nation, and a place where it is illegal to pump your own gas. On the downside, I was now surrounded by *more* fur balls. As the movers walked back and forth from the moving vans, two cats growled and sprayed the front steps of our new home. Our new neighbors came over and introduced one cat as "Jack Daniels" and the other as "Captain Morgan." They were hulking gray and black tabbies, the ward bosses of the neighborhood. From the beginning, we were warned that these cats were territorial and nasty but we dismissed their advice. We had cats and we knew how to handle cats so we scoffed at their warnings to our own peril.

The next morning, I had my first breakfast in our new house, kissed Melissa goodbye and proceeded on my way to work. Oscar and Dash were lined up to go out and discover their new territory. I knew they wanted to see if the chipmunks tasted the same here as in Connecticut. I opened the door and the ward bosses were standing like two sphinxes, hissing and positioned to claw the eyes of whatever dared to come on their turf. All three cats crouched low, ears back and tails flipping angrily as a low menacing growl rumbled deep in their chests. Oscar and Dash twitched their bottoms, ready to pounce but stopped short of an actual confrontation; they knew they had met their match. Melissa came to the door, sized up the situation, and blurted out, "Reprobates" then shooed them off the stoop and booted our cats out the door. I began to use the name; it *fit*.

A couple of days later, we drove to enroll Craig at his new school. Our new neighbor was getting her newspaper as Jack Daniels and Captain Morgan affectionately rubbed against her ankles. We stopped to chat, and from the backseat, Craig piped up, "Look, Mommy, the Reprobates." Our very nice new neighbor looked from Craig to me and couldn't decide whether she was more amused or offended at my family's opinion of her cats. Melissa muffled a laugh and I fumbled with the gears. When we pulled away, we looked at each other and laughed, proud of Craig for talking and "getting it." We took it as another sign that everything was going to be all right in New Jersey.

Every morning, the Reprobates guarded the outdoors from our interloping cats and, every morning, Melissa shooed them away, protecting her three furry children. However, the word "sucker" still blinked on her forehead. More than once, I caught her putting food and water on the stoop for those terrors. My adorable Melissa would pet these two animals even though she had been warned against it many, many times. Sure enough, I came home to find her on the front porch fighting with Captain Morgan, blood gushing everywhere. I couldn't decide whether Melissa or the Reprobate was screaming the loudest. I saw his brownish white claw deeply embedded in her hand and we almost had to have it surgically removed. Did she learn her lesson? Nope. The next night she attempted, once more, to pet Captain Morgan. Was I surprised? Not anymore. My woman had scratches all over her arms from her wrists to her elbows, and I knew it would never have occurred to Melissa to stop petting those horrible beasts. And I thought my travails would be limited to the cats I actually owned.

One evening, Melissa and I were invited next door for dinner. As we slipped between the prickly hedges of roses that separated our properties, we wondered how Captain Morgan and Jack Daniels would treat us, especially since we were going to be on their turf. As we were welcomed in, I discovered two possible explanations as to why the Reprobates were so mean: Scarlet and Rebecca, two silky and imperious Birmans, poised like queens on the settee, and I saw Robert perched comfortably in Mom and Dad's lives.

"Where's Captain and Jack?" asked my wife, always a glutton for punishment.

"Oh, we never let them in," said my neighbor. "Since my daughter returned from college with her cats, they peed all over everything and they've been outside ever since."

I recognized the Reprobates' jealousy and isolation, warming up to them, *just a little*. So when the weather turned bitter cold and Melissa began to sneak in Captain Morgan and Jack Daniels, I held my tongue. Usually, they would just run up the stairs and sleep in the guest bedroom, but if they were discovered, especially by Oscar, then pandemonium would reign. Then, there was the matter of my cashmere sweater.

"Melissa, this has got to stop. They're terrorizing our cats."

"I can't just leave them out there," she said blushing trying to hide her scratched arms.

"But they pissed on my sweater. Damn it, Melissa," I said holding the sweater between a pinched thumb and forefinger.

"I won't let them in anymore," she lied.

"I bet you won't pet them anymore, either. How long do outdoor cats live?"

Her eyes widened, taking in my full meaning. I had won this battle and the Reprobates were expelled from the house but still held sway out of doors.

Not long after moving into our New Jersey home, I began to feel the same magnetism I had felt living in our apartment in the Theo's building in New York. I became aware that it is not where you live but who you are with and what energy is following you. I knew from the very beginning this location was ordained, just like my apartment in Murray Hill. As I breathed the air, I knew something special was going to happen here. And it did. The very next day while Melissa was reading the paper in the family room with her glasses off (as she normally did), a huge hulking mass of blackish brown fur walked across our north patio.

"What a big dog. That's too big to be Boomer," said Melissa, referring to our neighbor's dog. Melissa put on her glasses and jumped out of her seat, yelling, "It's a bear, Dean. A bear! And the cats ... they're outside."

Many people in New Jersey would not regard a bear sighting as an unusual occurrence, but to ex-city slickers like us, it was really exciting. I ran downstairs and opened the door to the back deck just wide enough to let Oscar run in and Dash to bolt out and rush the bear.

"Do something," said Melissa. "Oh, Dash!"

Out the window, I saw that Dash's back was up like a camel's hump, his teeth bared, and his tail was like a flagpole. I was torn between being proud of Dash's bravery and appalled by his stupidity. Luckily for Dash, the young bear wasn't interested in a crazy cat and only wanted the tasteless salmon burgers I had just thrown in the garbage can. Melissa dialed 911, reported the bear, and her jaw dropped as she said, "I don't want you to shoot him!"

"Oh my God," I shook my head.

"Oh, *shoo* him," said Melissa. "Okay, officer. I thought you said shoot." She hung up. "Dean, they're coming to shoo the bear," she said, then frowning. "But that means the bear could come back and Craig plays out there."

We didn't know whether to laugh or cry so we decided to laugh. All the signs pointed to another *rabbit hole* and who knew Morristown, NJ would be host to bears, turkeys, coyotes, possums, raccoons, ground hogs, bats, and, of course, pissing cats. Being with Melissa, I was in another vortex, on another one way journey with the path clearly marked by furry paws, large and small.

CHAPTER 31
TRIPOD

Some people live in perfect harmony without animals or pets intruding into their lives. The suburbs brought us many new experiences, including the afternoon when Melissa discovered a baby bird on our front yard. For the next three hours, I drove to a raptor rescue center, where they cared for abandoned baby birds, instead of sitting on my back deck with a beer. It seemed that animals instinctively knew where to find us. Once again, we were on their radar, and today we would meet the cat that fell from the sky.

So far, it had been a great summer. Our tomato garden had yielded so much fruit, we all had canker sores, and the deer and rabbits hadn't eaten all the blueberries off the bushes that bordered our back yard. Today, we decided to eat breakfast on our deck. Pulling out the griddle, I cooked bacon, eggs, and blueberry pancakes. While we were eating this delicious meal, we heard a very faint "meow" coming from beneath the deck.

"Did you hear that?" said Melissa.

"No, not a thing" I said, knowing damn well I heard a cat. It was so loud the second time it meowed it may as well have been a car alarm.

"I heard it," said Craig.

"Meeeooow."

"It's under the deck," said Melissa with a big smile. "I'll get some food to temp it out."

Underneath the deck was a very young kitten, shaking and trying to hide. Melissa, of course, got all mushy-eyed while I just stood there, scratching my head. Why me? I was relishing my grilled breakfast and some quiet time with my family, and now I had to deal with this. Since our move to New Jersey, Melissa had been too busy getting our new house in order to even contemplate getting a fourth cat. Now, she didn't need to bother; it appeared that fate delivered.

Melissa placed a bowl of water and wet food under the deck and eventually coaxed the kitten out of hiding. Here we go again, another bathroom barricaded just like when Melissa brought home Sammy and Timmy. To our horror, we saw large open wounds on the kitten's hind quarters and that it was limping, possibly due to a broken leg. Trying to make sense of the kitten's injuries, we thought that a large bird, perhaps a hawk, had snatched the grey feral kitten from its litter and accidently dropped its meal in our backyard. While Melissa worried about the rest of the litter, I cursed the clumsy bird that apparently answered to a higher authority, the one insisting I will always be stuck with four cats.

Why four? It reminded me of when I was working in Rome and there were four of us on the assignment. Pope John Paul I had just died, and every night after work, we hailed a cab to take us to the Vatican. Some of us were Catholic and some were not; that did not matter. We were a part of history and stood silent in our own worlds as we waited for the white smoke signaling, as it had for centuries, the election of a new pope. After several evenings of standing in Saint Peter's Square, our feet hurt and we were growing increasingly tired of being jostled by the burgeoning crowds until we looked up and saw smoke. At first, no one could make out if the smoke was white or black. The sun had set long ago; eventually we heard someone in the crowd of thousands say, "Look, its white. We have a new pope."

The energy in the crowd was incredible and I actually became connected to it. Within the hour, the new pope, John Paul II, stepped up to the big window and issued his first blessing in numerous languages. I sensed that this was no coincidence. I was a part of history and beginning to feel the threads of connection.

A couple of years after my visit to Rome, I found a psychic who told me that in my past life I had been a Roman senator. Because of my experience, it felt very real and plausible. Of course, everyone wants to hear that in their past lives they were a great artist, famous ball player, statesmen or member of a royal family. No one wants to hear that they used to be the "royal ass wiper" at Versailles trailing behind *le roi* with a bowl and towel. This certainly made me think twice before I complained about my current job. So, four seems to always be my number, whether I like it or not.

Truly, it was never going to end. If it wasn't raining birds from the trees, then it was raining cats from the sky. And this was cat number seven! Never mind that it interrupted a wonderful breakfast; it ruined the day (and possibly the rest of the summer) because I had no doubt the next two to three weeks our lives would be devoted to the care of this tiny intruder.

After a quick look under the kitten's tail, Melissa decided that the kitten was a female and was thrilled to have another female in our testosterone-laden household. On the way to the vet, she named the cat, "Lily" and Craig bounced up and down in his car seat, excited to have a new friend. Melissa handed Lily over to the vet, and then joined Craig and me in the waiting room while the kitten was being examined. In about an hour, the vet joined us, an estimate in his hand, and explained the extent of Lily's injuries. I took one look at the exorbitant bill and knew we would have to sell our house and move into a tent to save the kitten's broken leg. With a few sharp breaths and *looks* in Melissa's direction, I showed her the bill. Melissa returned my looks with some of her own and told the vet to proceed. The vet informed us that there was no guarantee that the kitten would survive; we had to take it day by day. He also added that Lily was actually a boy and if we had we not found him when we did, the kitten would have been dead within 24 hours. None of us could have faced another death, especially after losing Sammy barely a year ago.

On the way home, I suggested we rename the cat "Lucky" and the rest of my family agreed. *Finally*, I got to name a cat. Despite Lucky's miraculous recovery, the kitten's delicate leg bones were shattered beyond repair and the only real option was to amputate the front left leg, thus making this kitten the most expensive FREE cat I have ever owned.

We were told many cats with three legs climb trees and play just like all the others. And they were right; we marveled at how fast Lucky could run. We also bestowed on him nicknames such as "Tripod" and "Lucker." We loved the cat, but worried about his future, just as we had done before with Timmy and Sammy, who all had feral beginnings. Though affectionate to Craig, Lucky preferred hiding to interacting with humans, opting to spend his days in the drop ceiling of our basement. Soon after we paid off Lucky's thousand dollar vet bill, the sink in our powder room started to leak and our friend, Gerry, who's a plumber, agreed to take the job. As Gerry removed the drop ceiling tiles in our basement, in order to examine the pipes, a pair of bright green eyes unexpectedly looked back at him from within the dark overhead space. Not knowing if this was a raccoon, or worse, Gerry screamed and fell backwards off his ladder. Shaken but unharmed, he went home to change his underwear while Lucky started to socialize more with the other cats, particularly with Onion, who loved to jump on a kitchen chair and dangle his tail in front of Lucky so the youngster could swat at it.

After all these years, there was no question in my mind that Melissa has an invisible neon tattoo on her forehead that said "SUCKER" and only cats and vets could see it. Underneath was inscribed: Give me your tired, your whiskered, your poor and hungry (my husband pays for vet care).

CHAPTER 32
A PARALLEL UNIVERSE

The first week of September, Melissa and I took in Craig to his new pre-school. Like Connecticut, the students had a myriad of differing diagnoses. Unlike Connecticut, Craig was more settled and a bit more socialized; still, we both knew he was lonely. There were no children his age in the neighborhood and we had few contacts in the area outside of my employment. Melissa suggested that we throw a party inviting Craig's classmates and parents. "Let's create an underground world for our son," she said, "so life doesn't pass him by."

We began by hosting a Halloween party and every child from his class was invited. Most of the children arrived with one or both of their parents in tow, who stayed for the entire party just in case their child had a meltdown. We spared no expense on spider webs, orange lights, masks, pumpkins, and games. There was a ton of toilet paper in the basement so kids could wrap each other as mummies and look at themselves in mirrors. Everyone ran a relay race with plastic eyes balanced in spoons. We brought in a petting zoo. Twelve barnyard animals roamed in a small gated area in our front yard: chickens, goats, rabbits, even a llama. This was the first party some of these kids had ever been invited to. One child just stood inside the portable petting zoo holding a goat by its leash, looking as life could not have offered anything sweeter.

A demure mother with slumped shoulders said to me and Melissa, "Please forgive my daughter's behavior," when the girl screamed and jerked on the swings.

"Don't worry," I said. "You and your child are safe here. No one is judged and everyone understands what you are going through. Short of setting us on fire, we're cool. You are welcome at our home and we hope you keep coming back."

The mother, almost in tears, touched my arm and looked into my eyes. I could see her pain and recognized it as our own. I was warmed by her gratitude, and from my eyes, I saw a tiny puncture in the *veil*, knowing we were on the right path. Melissa and I created a wormhole of acceptance, rescuing others like ourselves. Later, I was sitting out back away from the crowd. Fluffy clouds reached like mountains into the blue sky. I was humbled; we had changed their worlds and ours for the better. We, like our guests, were not alone.

The parties became tradition: Christmas, Easter, Halloween, Craig's birthday, picnics. During that first party, we all hovered over our children, torn between delight at their happiness and fear that it would be too much for them. The next party was for Craig's birthday when the kids ate in the dining room with minimal parental hovering. By the following Easter, the kids ate their pizza in the family room while watching *Veggie Tales* and the parents actually ate more adult fare, no hovering at all.

We had created our own circle of friends and it did not matter if a couple of neighborhood yahoos chose to sneak by our front yard trying to avoid us. Their behavior was irrelevant as we watched Craig grow in this new loving world that we had a part in creating. As Craig socialized more, he became less rooted in parallel play; we saw more mingling and interaction with the other children. As the parties progressed, Craig's sociability increased. In time, many of the children who comprised the original circle moved on to "typical" classrooms, while others needed specialized schools.

The gyroscope of life continued to amaze me as we adjusted our radar and moved according to the path we had chosen. My heart swelled when I came home from work and heard Melissa singing to Craig and I watched his hopeful eyes looking at his mommy. As people whose value had not been seen or appreciated in our childhood, Melissa and I were well equipped to offer Craig all that we had missed. Like Onion adjusting to Melissa's movements during sleep, when he always made sure to stay the course. The universe had given us a chance to give to Craig what we ourselves never received: unconditional love.

Autism by definition means you have very limited social skills, as that part of the brain is blocked off, and Craig, therefore, reacted to things in mechanical ways. But, despite his disability, he was brilliant.

A popular depiction of a nerd was a kid who's socially and physically awkward, yet very smart, and Craig was a nerd. I smiled knowing that the world has typically been changed by so-called nerds.

CHAPTER 33
A NEW HOMEROOM IN EARTH SCHOOL

After a particularly grueling day, I arrived home from work, cold and tired. As I walked to the door, I noticed that the porch lights were off, which was unusual. I put my key in the lock and the front door was already open, a sure sign that something was wrong. Last year, Craig had been placed a "typical" class with an aide. Though he had some rough patches, we hoped everything would work out. Melissa greeted me at the door; she was holding back tears and her voice shook as she told me Craig had hit his aide and was expelled from school. Dropping my keys and briefcase, my lips were thin and my stomach was in knots. No longer able to hold back the tears, Melissa said, "Its March; we have to wait until September to get him back into school." I held her and tried to calm her sobs, knowing mine were just below the surface.

The next morning, Melissa began searching for a special needs school that would meet all of Craig's needs. With patience and persistence, she found a private special education school in Bergen County and Craig was accepted. In order to help ease the transition, the school district dispatched a variety of tutors for Craig. One observed him for fifteen minutes and announced (in front of Craig) that she didn't realize he was so profoundly handicapped and left. Another tutor, eschewed academics and devoted his time teaching Craig how to play chess. The tutor's methodology revolved around besting our seven year-old son at every game. Aware of Craig's growing frustration, Melissa suggested that it would be better if he taught Craig *how* to play. On this point and many others, they butted heads, and, within a couple of weeks, he sailed out the door, also never to return.

The long months of summer finally passed and a new school year was beginning. We held Craig's hands and walked into his new classroom. Arts and crafts materials lined the room, a saltwater fish tank held clown fish and anemones, bookcases packed with colorful books lined the room, paper cups filled with dirt were waiting for the kids to sow seeds, and a loose configuration of desks and cushions furnished the room. The school even had a therapy dog named, Laddie, that paid a visit to each class every day. Craig's new teacher, Linda, was smiling as the children began the first day back to school. My heart rested and stress ran out of me like winged tendrils flying away leaving me light and giddy. My child was safe. Once again, we have gone full circle and life began anew. We now had a fresh start with a fighting chance.

CHAPTER 34
SOMETIMES THE END IS NOT THE END

Theo and I had worked together for 20 years. We had spoken on the phone daily, sometimes for hours, and this was my side job. We had shared life secrets, pains, heartaches and joys. Because he was a psychologist, our conversations were like therapy. We were best friends even though we had only seen each other four times in our lives. Theo's impact on my life rested right behind Melissa's. He was a voice on the phone, invisible yet critical to my survival. Like God, he was a powerful force I never saw.

Theo said he learned things from me as well. He used to take some of my theories to the local general store in his small New England town, where friends hung out every morning for coffee. He would mention *Earth School*, the universal order of things, cats with souls, guides, and the *veil*. Then we would talk as he shared his friends' remarks. We would shift from business to theology on a dime, making Theo laugh at my dexterity of mind. Melissa also laughed at my dexterity of mind but for very different reasons.

Thank God, Theo was a lifelong cat person and one of the few people I knew who appreciated my nearly inexhaustible supply of stories about feline antics. He was also a philanthropist for many charities, but as he became more and more disappointed in the virtues of the human race, he donated considerable funds to animal shelters that catered to cats. One day, I received an ominous call from him.

"Dean, I have some news for you." His voice was somber. "The doctor tells me I have cancer. Pancreatic."

I couldn't say anything. The air had been knocked out of my lungs, just like at the barn so many years ago.

"I'm going to fight this thing," said Theo. "I'll be admitted to Sloan Kettering tomorrow, the best in the business."

Light inside my head went dark and time stopped. My anchor. "I'll do whatever you need me to do," I said. "Whatever."

"Good, thank you. Dean ... I'd like to ask you to be the executor of my will."

"Executor? Theo, I …"

"Now wait. I can't put this burden on my wife, and, I trusted you with my most valuable assets, my buildings, all these years. Please, Dean, you said, 'whatever.'"

"Yes, sure I will. But let's not talk about this now. Let's get you healthy," I said knowing full well that this was unlikely.

"Dean, I need your word that you'll take this on."

"You have my word, Theo. You know you can rely on me." I tried to contain my hopelessness. My energy expanded beyond my skin as if I was trying to reach him. His voice held death. My thoughts froze and I relied on instinct to continue the conversation knowing that anyone with pancreatic cancer had three months, at most, knowing my world had changed in the blink of an eye, knowing I was going to lose my friend.

I didn't want to have the void of childhood back in my life. Theo accepted me, and our conversations had allayed feelings of loss, abandonment, pain that haunted me for so many years. I wanted the connection, the friendship, to continue forever. I had watched his Aunt die and now I was destined to watch Theo travel the same path. I briefly flashed back to the image of my grandmother in her casket with her eyes sewn shut. Death haunted me.

The phone rang the next day and I barely recognized Theo's voice. It had dropped a full octave and every word he uttered seemed to be a herculean effort.

"Dean, I need to ask you something." I could hear his labored breathing and I didn't know what to do. "I can't get into Sloan Kettering for two more weeks. I can't bear the pain."

"Theo, you have money. Isn't there another treatment center? And why can't you get proper medication to alleviate the pain?"

"The cancer is around my esophagus," he labored, "I can't ingest the pills. My doctor's getting an IV delivered tomorrow."

Almost dropping the phone, I'm shook my head. "I am so sorry, Theo."

Knowing there are no words of comfort I asked, "How are your cats?"

Theo chuckled appreciating the diversion. "Fine. How's that Dash? Still hanging around Craig?"

"Yeah, they're funny together." Theo knew I would be his friend to the end.

After he checked into Sloan Kettering, I found an attorney who was willing to go to his hospital room so Theo could sign important documents to settle his affairs. Decisions had to be made about who would get his assets and how much. I was there to implement his wishes. I did the same for Ruth before she died. The next day at work, I got a call from Sheri, a woman who used to live around the corner of Theo's main building.

"Sheri, is that you?" I said. "It's been a while." She was a drop dead gorgeous brunette with long legs and a lithe body. For some reason, I sat up straighter and pulled in my gut.

"I know this is awkward and you probably don't know that Theo and I have been … intimate … for some time now." (I always knew she wanted to marry money.) "I know his wife is with him in the hospital, so I am hoping you will do me a favor."

"What is it?"

"Please tell him that I love him. I want him to know before he dies."

My hand shook as I placed the receiver in its cradle. I never suspected, not for an instant. All these years, I thought Theo and I knew each other. Slumped in my desk chair, I picked up a pen and filled a piece of paper with swirls and circles. Did I ever know him? For the next week, I kept Sheri's phone call from Theo. Despite Theo's evident decline, when I spoke to him my voice was tinged with a bitterness I couldn't quell. It all came down to one simple fact: delivering Sheri's message was part of my job and I would play the good flunky.

When I told him, Theo became quiet and averted his eyes. I would never know if Sheri's confession had pleased him or made him angry. Silence prevailed as his wife walked into the room. I had noticed throughout the years that people close to death shut you out of their lives and purposefully make you angry. I didn't know if it was a conscious thing but I knew it happens. I think it was a way to break ties and give the living time to prepare for their demise. Part of me wondered if they were already partially on the other side of the *veil* and couldn't communicate with the living.

A few days later, after not hearing from Theo or his wife, I called.

"How is he?" I asked his wife.

"Dean, Theo passed." She started to cry.

"I am so sorry. When did he ... when is the service?"

"Oh, Dean," she said, "Theo has already been buried. There was no funeral, just a graveside service. Because of Thanksgiving, we made quick arrangements because ... it's our way, to bury loved ones immediately."

I didn't hear another word she said. For some reason, I remembered both Theo and Ruth died in cold months. An irrelevant thing to dwell on but I needed a diversion because my emotions were raw – twenty years and no phone call. I was empty; everything had changed and I was uncomfortable on planet Earth. Though reason pecked at my emotions, I wanted no part of it. I had been shunned and I was hurt.

That night Oscar slept on my pillow because he knew I needed him. I wondered about Theo's cats and realized I would never hear about them again. I missed them already. My deep connection to Theo and my experiences managing his buildings were gone. There was no sign at his death like there was with my grandmother and Ruth, no recurring dream, no light bulbs going out. It was over, final, and his loss was palpable. Just as my grandfather felt the urge scratch his toe, long after it had been removed, I still felt a connection, yet so much was unresolved.

Theo's estate eventually sold the buildings that I managed to a new owner, but the *rabbit hole* was not going to let me go just yet. The new owners decided that I was the best person, with the most experience, to continue running their buildings, and I agreed. Sometimes, when you think you are at the end, it ain't necessarily so.

CHAPTER 35
ONION AND SCALLION

During the last year, Onion had aged considerably. He was almost twenty, beating the average feline life expectancy by miles. His muzzle was peppered with white fur, and Melissa was assiduously monitoring his health, taking him to the vet almost every week. I sensed her growing depression even though Onion had lived a long, well-loved life.

"I don't want to be responsible for deciding whether or not to put another animal down. I can't do it," said Melissa.

I decided not to pressure her, but I knew Onion needed to go to the vet. Within two days, Melissa came into the family room where I was reading the newspaper. "I was walking up the stairs and prayed for a sign to tell me what to do because I can't bear to watch another one of my cats die. I don't have the strength. When I went into the bedroom, Onion crawled out from under the bed and had diarrhea all over the carpet; cats never do that."

I stood up and held her.

"I called the vet and talked to him," she said into my shoulder. "It's time to go."

My throat muscles tensed. Onion was an innocent creature and the first cat who adopted me. After so many years of being together, another part of me was going to the other side. We were both in the vet's office, and I overheard Melissa whisper into Onion's ear as she caressed his soft fur, "Go find Binky."

The first shot was administered, followed by the fatal second. Onion's body relaxed, and soon his breathing ceased. Melissa gently lifted Onion, cradling him in her arms, saying again and again, "I don't want to leave you." Later that night, Melissa looked at me square in the eyes and said,

"I was debating whether to tell you this but ... on the way back to the car at the vet's office, a voice spoke to me. I know it was the same voice that spoke to me when Fluffy, my cat in college died. It just said 'thank you.'" I know it was Onion.

Our Onion lived a full life and we were honored to be with him. The Onion had been there for me, and I respectfully mourned him with his official name—D'Artagnan. "May your passage to the other side be blessed," I said as we toasted our cherished cat.

Melissa had a way of adapting the cat's characteristics to songs. We both loved the song "Unforgettable" by Nat King Cole, and Melissa had been singing this for years so, in honor of our always famished cat, D'Artagnan, we sang:

> *Unfillable, that's what you are*
> *Unfillable, you are my star*
> *Like a pit that is bottomless*
> *You'll soon look like a Hippopotamus*
> *That is why you're so unfillable, now*

I recognized the irony of her words and how they pertained to us too, as we both hungered for love in our past.

♣

We are all a part of the life cycle, and death was just part of the deal. I didn't see it as evil; my grandmother taught me that. Death just is. Missing someone was such a privilege and perhaps the ultimate gift. The loss of Theo and Onion was a sign that it was my time to go it alone for a while. I had received the gift of their friendship and I would treasure it forever, but now it was time to move on. I needed to face life with a new perspective while holding onto the valuable lessons learned from these wonderful souls close to my heart.

Since Onion passed, Melissa and Craig needed another kitty and went on a quest. This reminded me of my grandfather's missing toe, bringing on a hankering to fill my void as well. Typically ignoring free cat emails, one caught my eye. Going against my policy of not telling Melissa about these free cats, this time I brought a copy home and handed it to her. There was a feral litter living in a wooded patch near a co-worker's backyard. Melissa flew to her car and sped off, returning in what seemed like seconds. Melissa had chosen her eleventh cat (including the three she had before she met me) from

Nature's bounty. Once again, another *free* kitten came knocking at my door.

My first inclination was to name the kitten "Corn" but Melissa refused, citing that he wasn't yellow and I knew this was just an excuse to get another cat in the future. I read somewhere that during its life, each adopted cat cost their owner about eleven thousand dollars. I quickly calculated that I was about one hundred and twenty one thousand dollars in the hole due to Melissa's mania for cats, *lucky me.* Feeling rebellious, I insisted that we keep the vegetable-cat name game alive, in honor of Onion, so we settled on "Scallion," whose black fur sported a white bib.

He reminded me of Sammy when he first came into my life, so small and playful. He was delightful with Craig, and I knew we did the right thing. Three weeks later, on a warm sunny summer morning, while I was deep in concentration, my office phone rang. Melissa, almost incoherently, said, "Scallion is dead!"

"My God, what happened?"

"Craig, Scallion and I were outside waiting for Craig's school bus," she sobbed into the phone. "It was such a beautiful day ... and the flowers ..."

"Melissa, what happened?"

"I let Scallion come out with Craig to wait for his bus. They were running around playing. Scallion was so cute and curious. I wanted Craig to have some time with him before he went to school ... with just losing Onion. After Craig got on the bus, I saw Scallion out of the corner of my eye running after him. Then everything was a blur. Tires screeched, I screamed, and ..." she choked, "Scallion screamed. He was under the bus wheel." The phone dropped.

"Melissa, Melissa," I paced, loosening my tie. "Melissa!"

With a clatter in my ear, I heard, "Dean, it was awful! Craig saw everything. It's my fault, my fault."

"I'm coming home," I yelled and hung up. I avoided the questioning glances and told my secretary I had a family emergency.

I pulled up just as the school counselor arrived. It was almost too much to bear knowing that Craig had witnessed the death of our new kitten. I looked up for comfort and saw puffy clouds that reminded me of angels. Desperate for higher meaning, I saw the blue sky mixed with the clouds and thought of the *veil*. I wanted it to burst through. This slow march to death and beyond was killing me. I was fully aware that there would be more pain to come. That evening, Melissa placed a picture of Scallion as a memorial at the top of our stairs. She was full of guilt and I approached and wrapped my arms around her.

"It's not your fault," I said.

Even though Scallion was in our lives for only a brief time, those precious days were significant and would be cherished. Craig was getting bigger daily but today he was forced to grow up fast. I watched him make another passage along life's journey joining with me and Melissa while the remaining cats in our household, sensing the tragedy, began to fill the void just as water penetrates the crevices in a dam. Once again, life went on and we proceeded to fill our purpose. Scallion's short life reminded me that our time allotted here on Earth was very precious; we had to fulfill our destinies before it became too late.

A month later, Melissa and I snuggled in bed. Just before sleep, small footfalls pounced on the bed.

"Did you feel that?" I asked Melissa.

"I felt something ... one of the cats?"

I looked down. No cats. And the bedroom door was shut.

"I wasn't going to tell you, but it happens a lot," Melissa said. "It's Bink or Onion."

"Or Sammy or Scallion," I added.

"Or Timmy."

We laughed looking into each other eyes, connecting; I felt calm and a deep, wonderful sleep ensued. Again, *Earth School* dictated that we take a recess to process the lessons of the day.

CHAPTER 36
PETER THE "BELLY SLUT" AND FLY

In the 60's, John Lennon wrote a song on the *White Album* called "Number 9." We were at Number 11 with Scallion and I knew it wouldn't stop there. After the tragedy of Scallion, Melissa got the urge to fill the household quota. Cuddling up to me on the couch, she kissed my cheek. Folding her legs under her, she burrowed in. I put the newspaper aside. Craig was watching his favorite cartoon, *SpongeBob*, but when he saw Melissa and me, our boy decided to join the snuggle fest on the couch.

"Dean, I need another kitty," said Melissa.

Craig smiled; he knew his mother well. Here we go again, I thought, rolling my eyes. But her face so close and her soft eyes unnerved me. I kissed her and she knew she had me. Forever and a day, she had me. The next day, while I was at work, they sneaked off to a shelter.

"Look Daddy, this is Peter," said Craig holding the kitten with pride.

"He reminds me of Binky," I said, leaning down to pet his black fur. "What's wrong with his eye?"

"Oh that," said Melissa, keeping herself busy not making eye contact. "It was badly infected when he was born so the shelter had to remove it."

I straightened up to see if she was kidding, but she was busy fussing with dishes that didn't need to be rearranged.

"I see the savior has yet not retired," I said, in a soft voice causing Melissa to finally look at me. I smiled and relaxed; what a gentle soul I had married. "I love you," I mouthed the words. *The Mother Ship* landed once again reminding me that Sammy also had an infected eye. This time, we got a solid black cat with little angel kisses on his neck. There were about twelve white hairs scattered in a cluster, barely enough to get the cat out of the Halloween bad luck category. Since he reminded me of the Black Bear, I started calling him "The Cub" as a tribute to Binky.

I warmed up to him instantly, and he jumped up in my lap. Peter clearly knew we rescued him, but I wondered if he would ever know how really lucky he was to have been chosen by such a loving family. I started to rub his jaw just the way I used to do with Robin.

"Dean, look. Every time this cat comes over, he flops on his back with paws in the air as if to say, 'Rub my belly, he says," she said, "My little *Belly Slut.*"

As she rubbed his belly, he bit her hand. Melissa called these love nips and continued to pet him. It reminded me of telling Melissa that Onion would let her rub him until he was raw. I think she actually did rub some of his hair off at one point.

You knew we had a new cat when Melissa concocted a new song. To the tune of "Santa Claus is coming to town" she sang:

> *You better not flinch,*
> *You better not whine,*
> *You better not cry, I 'm telling you why,*
> *Cause Peter Parker's going to bite.*

Chorus

> *He'll bite you when you're sleeping*
> *He'll bite you when you're awake.*
> *He'll bite you whether you been good or bad*
> *He'll just bite no matter what … (repeat)*

Most people would have thrown the cat out but my honey memorialized their neurotic behavior in song. After she sang her song, I looked over at her smiling face and said, "You know Melissa, this cat is just like the Bink without the Stink!" If I didn't know better, I thought she had flipped me the bird for that comment but I soon found out that Peter thought I smelled bad. Each time I would touch or pet Peter, he immediately gave himself a bath. I was so offended but Craig got a kick out of it and would bring Peter over to me insisting that I pet him just to see Peter give himself another bath.

My kind wife said, "At least that animal has taste."

Often before going to sleep, I would listen to music on my iPod. While I listened to The Black Eye Peas, Peter came close pretending he was going to rub up against me. He approached slowly, each paw deliberately placed one in front of the other like I was prey, but instead of loving cuddles, he bared his teeth and attacked my earphone cord. I admit that I did wonder with amusement what would have happened if the cord had been electric.

"What next?" I said to Melissa who watched with amusement. Now I had to keep both eyes open as I slept, one for Melissa and her gonad removing knife from the vet, and the other for cats trying to eat my personal property. When I woke up the next morning, as karma did its thing, now it was my turn as Peter curled his body like a turban around my head. His whiskers penetrated one ear while his tail was sticking in the other. Every morning, I awoke looking like a disheveled pasha, but Melissa, who refused to recognize my lordship, had different ideas.

"I see you like to wear bonnets behind my back? Is there anything else I should know about?"

"Nice."

The next night, I saw Melissa but couldn't believe my eyes because her hair had turned from red to black. In my disorientation, I realized that Peter had completely surrounded her head from ear to ear.

"Why are you wearing a bonnet in the bed?" I inquired as I woke Melissa.

"Oh this," she said. "He has been doing this all night. I couldn't sleep a wink. Tonight we are having a cat free night."

"I'll believe it when I see it. At least you know he loves you!" I said laughing. "From now on we are going to call him "The Bonnet.'"

Another name for Peter was the "Corsage Kitty" because he climbed up while I was reading or watching TV and positioned himself like a corsage by curling up around my neck blocking my view. If he could, he would have crawled inside me and burrowed in between my vital organs. But even I understood that the cat needed a connection just like all of us.

Just as I was getting used to all our cats, Dash, our *cow cat*, walked
into our bedroom and, instead of jumping on our bed, slept under
it. Melissa turned to me with worried eyes and said, "He looks old;
all his spots are grey."

I turned off the light and wrapped my arms around her. "The vet
tomorrow?" I asked but she didn't answer.

In the morning, I looked under the bed for my slippers, but Dash
didn't look up.

"Hon, something is wrong with Dash."

Like so many kitties before him, Dash now had weekly appointments
with our vet, who by now probably owned a summer house, that I
paid for, in Spring Lake. Once again, Melissa bought special cat food
and crammed pills down his throat. All her ministrations bought
him a few extra months, but, in the end, the answer was always going
to be the same.

"How are we going to tell Craig?" said Melissa as tears fell down
her cheeks. "Dash had such a strong connection with Craig. He
was Craig's connection to the world. We owe everything to this cat."

"You realize we have to get another cat immediately," I said, amazed
at the words I had just uttered from my mouth as well as my heart.
Melissa laughed through her tears.

A few weeks later, I walked in the door that night from a long day
at work. Craig, older at this point and much more verbal, ran up
with a big smile on his face and said, "Look Daddy, I picked this cat
out all by myself and named him 'Fly.'"

"Like his mother before him," I said as Melissa wiped her hands on
a dish towel. Our eyes met. "Why did you name him Fly?"

"Because, like Dash, he's *fast*."

Fly was our second tabby after Tripod. I reached over to pet him
and thought this cat's fur feels like a Brillo pad. Of course, I told
Melissa later that my nickname for Fly was "Brillo" but she was not
going to let that happen. I had to think of a special name because
tabbies look like miniature leopards but knew I could never top
Onion. I comforted myself with the thought that at least he had
four legs, two eyes and his original plumbing.

When Fly was outside, Melissa called at the top of her lungs for him to come in, but he didn't always respond. One night I said to Craig,

"Want to see Mommy go nuts?"

Craig nodded with a big smile.

"Open the door when Mommy is in the kitchen and call for Brillo and see if Fly shows up."

"OK, Daddy," said Craig, and bedlam would visit the Parker household that evening.

Fly grew to be a handsome young cat with a fully developed sense of humor. He was a big tease who loved to stand outside our sliding glass doors and stare at us with big sad eyes as if to say, "Let me in. Hurry up before one of the Reprobates eats me alive!" Of course, when we opened the door, Fly would turn, flip his middle claw and run away. Tired of being comedic fodder for a cat, I, being an intelligent but fundamentally lazy person, stopped rising to the bait, but dear Melissa continued to answer Fly's call and wonder why...

At first, Fly (or "It's me, Flea") could not stand the sight of me. Whenever I entered a room, he would run out. I felt a bit unappreciated (what else was new?) but Fly was Craig's cat, assuming Dash's place in his life. Like Lucky, Fly was skittish and slept at the foot of Craig's bed. The only time I would see Fly was at his food bowl or when he wanted me to let him out in the morning as I left for work. Fly would dart out and climb our arbor that was covered with a Trumpet vine. In summer, its limbs fashioned a cool green cathedral ceiling that was adorned with orange flowers, a natural magnet for hummingbirds. Every morning as I got in my car, I saw him climb up, camouflage himself behind the leaves, and wait for his prey. As I began a brand new meaningless day at the office, I thought of Fly and the delight on that cat's face that was second to none, as he waited for hours to claim his trophy(ies). When it rained or Fly was sleepy, he spent his day inside happily "making muffins" as he kneaded Melissa's lap. Our family understood each other's quirks, and we helped our cats along their path, just as they helped us along ours.

As I walked in from a long day at the office, the first thing I heard was Melissa saying, "I used to have a glamorous job in the city but now, I am a servant for the cats."

"I never grow weary of listening to you complain."

Then I saw Fly and Tripod marching down the steps as I went up to change. Melissa though I was out of earshot, when she began singing to the tune of Bringing in the Sheaves:

> *Tabbies on Parade, Tabbies on Parade,*
> *We shall come rejoicing, voicing*
> *Tabbies on Parade.*

"I heard that," I said while taking off my tie. Craig laughed and joined in the song.

A few years later, on a cold, snowy New Year's Day, Fly was at the door asking to come in. Craig yelled, "Fly is limping!" and we let him in thinking it was nothing more than a sprained paw, but soon Fly fell on his side, his breathing labored. Because of the holiday, we rushed Fly to an emergency veterinary hospital where we learned that he had passed a clot from his hind leg to his heart and suffered a heart attack. Fly was young, slender and fit; we never saw it coming.

"Your cat has a serious heart condition," the vet said. "You have the option of further tests and medication for the rest of his life or putting him down. I am very sorry but I must let you know that his chances are not good."

"Just like Timmy," said Melissa.

"I know. Let's get him some medicine and take him home."

Modern medicine is amazing because Fly lived another 16 months and Melissa had a new full time job as a nurse, sticking humongous pills down the poor animal's throat three times a day. "The savior," I thought each time I saw the chase. She had to hold down the cat, push the pill into its mouth, followed by a small sip of water then gently massage his neck so he would swallow.

"You're a mean mommy," I teased. "Look how red your arm is from holding that Brillo pad."

"I hate you."

"You're really a good mommy for pilling that cat. If only Fly understood that."

Melissa finally discovered cat pill pockets (these marketing people don't miss a trick) that came in assorted flavors such as chicken or duck, his favorite. You could put the pills in them making the cat think you were giving him food. Melissa called them "treats." Now I heard morning, noon, and night, "Fly, eat your treats!" Usually, Fly complied but every once in a while he refused so Melissa had to resort to the original, tried and true method. As I watched this drama play on day and after day, I realized that, all those years ago, I had chosen the right woman.

CHAPTER 37
THE MESSENGER

Today was the day we had prayed for but also feared. We left Craig with neighbors and drove to Melissa's parents' home to take them to the nursing home they so desperately needed. This was a bitter pill that was long overdue. For years, Melissa had begged them to sell their home and move into a place more suitable to their increasing states of disability but the answer had always been an unreasonable and defiant "no." Now, they had no choice. Melissa was distraught at the thought of witnessing their humiliation at being carried out of the home they had clung to with such tenacity and into a place where they wouldn't know anyone and strangers would be responsible for their every need.

As we pulled into their driveway, we saw that the minister from Jim's VFW post was already there as well as Jim's sister and her husband. I knew Melissa was grateful beyond words for their support because Evelyn and Jim bitterly resented Melissa, who had put her foot down when her parents announced, when we first moved to New Jersey, that they wanted to live with us. It was unthinkable for so many reasons but, most of all, because of Craig. Melissa was stretched to the breaking point but her parents were unconcerned; their needs came first. Relatives, whom she hadn't spoken to in years, showered her with calls stating, in no uncertain terms, that they would personally come to New Jersey and kick her ass if she allowed her parents to move in. They need not have worried; I knew they would have broken us beyond repair and I would not allow my family to be destroyed. What we did not know was how vicious their response would be.

♣

After we got her parents settled in their room, Melissa dropped me home and returned to the nursing home to complete the necessary paperwork. Even though it was a fine facility with lots of programs and activities, we all knew this would be their last stop on this planet. I wondered why she was even bothering. I knew the Fifth Commandment, honoring your father and mother and all that, but they didn't deserve it. They had proven that time and time again. They were using Melissa, and, I angrily thought, she chose to be complicit. Maybe I was being unfair, I knew the dilemma she faced but I couldn't think anymore. It had been a very long day, and I was grateful that our neighbors were keeping Craig through dinner. I decided to take a shower to wash away the musty smell of their unkempt house and the unmistakable odor of the nursing home when the phone rang. I wondered who in the world would be calling since our friends knew what we were doing today.

"Rosie," I said, surprised that Evelyn's best friend would call me. I never liked her very much. Her oily, unkempt hair always creeped me out but I was too tired to care; maybe, she wanted Evelyn's new phone number.

"What a surprise, Rosie," I said.

"I will just take a minute of your time," said Rosie. I could hear the anxiety in her voice. "Well, I know you are alone because Melissa is with her Mom. I just decided to pick up the phone and have a chat with you."

"Okay," I said, wondering what she could possibly have to say to me.

"Well, you know I am really good friends with Melissa's mother and we have talked about everything over the years. She is such a wonderful friend. I just think you should know that Evelyn has told me some things that I feel you need to know about."

"What are you talking about?" I asked.

"You must understand this is difficult for me. It all happened when Melissa was in high school. I just thought you should know."

"Know what?"

"Well, perhaps I shouldn't have called. I don't know how to say this."

"Rosie, just tell me."

"Alright, I called to tell you that Melissa and her father have been intimate."

My jaw dropped.

"Melissa and I have discussed this. I am fully aware of the situation and you are completely wrong."

I slammed down the phone as I tried to grasp the enormity of what just happened. I envisioned this bitch grinning on the other side of the phone and I knew she was lying. Evelyn had dispatched Rosie, as the messenger, to deliver her revenge. Was there no limit to her indecency? This was a carefully executed mission of destruction designed to replace desire with revulsion; to forge a chasm of suspicion and recrimination between Melissa and me; and to steal from our son the happy home he depended on to survive. Evelyn had declared war, wanting nothing less than the complete desolation of our family.

I really didn't care whether or not it was true as far as my relationship with Melissa was concerned. I loved Melissa which was something her parents clearly did not. There was something very sinister about that call; having contact with pure evil made me want another shower. I ran to the bathroom where I wretched this whole vile drama. About an hour later, Melissa walked in, tired and hoping for some comfort from a truly awful day.

"Have a seat." I said, "You've had a long day but I have something to tell you."

Completely shocked, Melissa looked at me with her beautiful green eyes and said, "I can't believe this. You must remember that I told you that my father made a pass at me when I was about twelve and that from that day on I slept a knife under my pillow. But I promise you, nothing ever happened!" I understood Melissa's defensiveness as she began to appreciate the gravity of what her mother had set in motion.

"I know and I absolutely believe you. I just want you to know what lengths your mother is willing to go to destroy our lives."

"My God," she said. "I am so humiliated. You and I both know Dad could be a pig but what has she told my relatives and friends? I'm calling Rosie, now."

But Rosie, as we both suspected, didn't have the guts to answer her phone.

"I'd like a martini; how about you?" I asked, glancing her way and seeing her smile. As I sipped my vodka and gin and chewed the olive, I thought about karma and wondered what form it would take as it shadowed Rosie for the rest of her life.

Melissa confronted her mother the next day and watched her squirm. Melissa told Evelyn that Rosie was never to call our house again and left it at that. How could Melissa tell her mother to stop telling lies about her having sex her own father, when he and her mother shared the same room? Evelyn had chosen her weapon well. The slightest innuendo of incest, let alone an outright accusation, will taint the innocent forever because how can they ever prove it never happened? I painfully observed that Melissa still wasn't ready to break all ties but I knew that nature would eventually lend a helping hand. It would only be a matter of time and we both had much more of that than they ever did. A sudden peacefulness came upon the house. The false prophet had come and gone and life would eventually go back to normal.

CHAPTER 38
AND THEN THERE WERE THREE

About two years later, we returned from a very relaxing vacation in Key West. On our way home from the airport, we stopped by the vet's office to pick up Peter and Lucky who were waiting for us in their kitty condos. Since Fly's death, life had been so busy that even Melissa was content with two cats. Unfortunately, our vacation must have invigorated her because, while I paid the bill, Melissa and Craig notice a sign in the office that said two tabby kittens needed a home and were available for adoption. How typical, I thought, we stopped in to collect Lucky and Peter and walked out with two more cats: Glacier, a silver-grey tabby, and his sister, Luna, a black and tan tabby. Once more, we have our limit of four cats and all is right with the world.

Before I got all the bags in the front door, the phone rang. I always let Melissa answer it, knowing it probably was her mother with a new tale of woe about Jim, the nursing home, the food, blah, blah, blah and blah. If the definition of crazy was doing the same thing over and over and expecting different results, then Melissa and I were certifiable. Somebody, get a net.

After Melissa hung up, I knew this was more than being on the receiving end of another bitch session from her mother. It was the nursing home and they wanted to discuss Hospice care for her mother. It seemed impossible, even though Evelyn had been sick for decades. In the past, she had always managed to pull the proverbial rabbit out of the hat, but not this time. I thought of Craig, who had lived through the deaths of Robin, Sammy, Scallion, Onion, Dash, and Fly, and wondered how he would react to something like this happening to his grandmother. Melissa went outside and quietly dead-headed all the flowers on our back deck; she didn't want to talk.

Late that night in our bedroom, Melissa and I wandered on to the topic of the first funeral I attended with her for her Uncle Alan. The funeral home was crowded with family and friends, grieving at Alan's passing but glad to be in each other's company. The casket was barely visible beneath all the loving tributes of roses, chrysanthemums and gladiolas. When the service started, we sat next to Melissa's cousin's wife, Darcy, and listened to the heartfelt speeches as we wiped away our tears and joined in the laughter which marked this very special goodbye. I became aware of something overhead. I raised my chin and looked up, feeling a presence above me, something of substance, yet without form or color. I looked at Melissa and she too had her eyes raised, looking for something. It was like a sixth sense, a fluttering of energy that was unmistakable, not subtle at all. At the end of the service, while congregating in the parking lot, Melissa gingerly broached the subject, "Okay, did you guys feel that?"

"Yes," said Darcy. "I thought it was just me."

"Me, too," I said, "I wasn't going to say anything."

We did not know who or what "it" was; maybe it was Uncle Alan checking up on who was at his funeral. I was sure that all three of us were near the threshold of the *veil*. Now, Melissa worried what aspect Evelyn would assume after her death.

The doctors gave Evelyn three months to live but three days later the phone rang; it was six in the morning. Melissa's voice cracked as she answered the phone and I knew it was time. There was no way to prepare Melissa for what would come. Evelyn had been teetering on the edge of death for over twenty years surviving several strokes, two heart surgeries, and numerous bouts of depression. Melissa always said, 'This is my mother's last Christmas ... last Mother's Day ... last birthday ..." you name it. I always said, "Your mother is immortal." Soon I would be proven wrong.

At first, Melissa's mother was conscious as they held hands. Jim drove his electric wheelchair in and out of her room but was incapable of staying very long. Melissa's father and mother no longer shared the same room. They had separated months before because of their constant arguing. Melissa left the room every time he visited to give them some privacy only to watch him depart ten or fifteen minutes later with her mother crying, "Where is he going?"

Other than Evelyn's surviving brother and his wife, who drove from Pennsylvania to say their goodbyes, Melissa was alone. By late afternoon, Jim stopped visiting and Evelyn began in earnest her journey to leave this world behind. Evelyn's breathing grew increasingly erratic and harsh. In her final hours, fluid gurgled in her throat until it breached the top, flooding her mouth, then receding, without a sound, back into her lungs; Melissa watched her mother drown.

Sadly, Evelyn died without ever reconciling the traumas of her past. In her delirium she murmured, "I'm sorry, Daddy," again and again. The little Melissa knew of her maternal grandfather was not good. He had deserted Evelyn's mother and their three young children to return to his "legitimate" family and never saw any of them again. The bastard wasn't worth a second thought, yet Evelyn had never reconciled his abandonment. In dying, some rise like a phoenix, their failures and triumphs integrated and layered like silky feathers, buoying them up as they fly while others are forever mired by the sorrow and disappointment This was Evelyn's real tragedy.

The next morning we collected her things at the nursing home and then drove to finalize her funeral arrangements, having no choice but to bring Craig with us. Prior to their entering the nursing home and in accordance with the nursing home's policy, residents had to pre-pay all funeral arrangements. So all Melissa needed to do now was drop off the pretty blue suit Evelyn had worn to our wedding, order flowers, and speak briefly with the funeral home's director. Aware that we wouldn't be spending much time with Craig over the next three days, we decided to take our deserving son to Great Adventure. From that point on, we jokingly called it "The Official Theme Park of Mourning." We were mindful of Craig and wanted to do everything we could to protect him from all this pain.

Before the funeral, my wife, being very astute, said, "I'll be dammed if I end up of changing my father's diapers during my mother's funeral." So she hired a nurse, and, sure enough, as soon as Jim's medical van pulled up to the funeral home, I heard him yell, "I just crapped in my pants, get Melissa over here now."

Without missing a beat, I called the nurse and made a mental note about just how smart my wife really was. I was so proud of Melissa for her insight and wisdom and at the same time very sorry for her on this awful day. Upon entering the funeral chapel, I noticed that there were only twelve people sitting in this oversized room with awkwardly placed chairs. The open casket was in the front surrounded by roses and lilies that wilted on this hot sticky July morning.

The minister from the VFW, who had stood by them when they moved, kindly offered to officiate. He was goodhearted and truly a man of God, but he was no public speaker. He bungled the Lord's Prayer and was so distraught we thought he was going to faint. Not one person sitting in that room dared make eye contact lest they lose their composure and burst out laughing. I saw karma in motion when I glanced around the room and saw horror on everyone's face. There was no "presence" as we had experienced at Uncle Alan's funeral; no uplifting of the *veil*. There always needs to be some sort of goodbye at a funeral. Here, there was nothing.

After the funeral, in order to add much needed levity to the situation, I told Melissa on the way home in the car, "You know that your mother is not in Heaven."

Melissa was too shocked to speak.

"Because," I said, "she is still at the Pearly Gates carping at Saint Peter about what a lousy husband she had since all he did was play golf when he was supposed to be taking care of her."

We burst out laughing, which I knew would start the healing process. Melissa had just been freed from a loveless, toxic bond. That night, we slept with all four cats and sometime during the night Melissa woke me saying she sensed an angry presence. "It was orange and red and climbing up the stairs. I know it was my mother," she said pulling the covers over her head.

"You were dreaming," I said, not quite believing what I was saying, but I knew the cycle had finished. I remembered the ghost in the basement apartment in New York and knew this was just as real to her. We never totally let go; influences from the past continue to linger on. The morning of 9/11, just after the plane crashed into the North Tower, Melissa rushed to the phone to call her mother. The receiver was in her hand before she remembered.

CHAPTER 39
TWO ...

When I got out of bed this morning, I tripped over an open suitcase. Craig's summer vacation began in two days and we would be on our way to the Grand Canyon. Sometime around noon as Melissa was icing cupcakes for a school party, the phone rang. Her father had suffered another stroke. By the time I got home that evening, James had already passed. I hugged Melissa as soon as I saw her at the door.

The funeral arrangements were much easier the second time. Everything was pretty much the same except there were no diapers to change. Melissa and I drove down her father's funeral, leaving her the only person alive in her immediate family. Each landmark Melissa spotted on the way down reflected memory after memory.

"That's the church where my parents were married," she said. "That's my high school."

I couldn't imagine how she was feeling. As before, I tried to think of ways to make her laugh as we waited in the parking lot just before the funeral. I tried to break the somber energy by telling a joke. She brushed me off, but I persisted and made up a scenario of her mom winning *Queen for a Day* by telling the saddest story about how awful her husband was. Melissa managed a weak smile, and I knew the only thing she wanted was for this day to end. What a blessing it is to mourn the loss of someone you love without reservation and celebrate a life well-lived. But this time, feelings were mixed and emotions were not our best friend.

Craig was home, once again, with our neighbors. In life, we had kept Craig away from Jim and Evelyn and saw no reason to inflict their deaths him now. Soon after they began living at the nursing home, Jim and Evelyn wanted to change their wills. While writing down their amendments, Melissa hesitantly asked her parents if they wanted to leave anything for Craig, their only grandchild. Jim's reply was, "Let Dean handle it. Craig is his responsibility, not mine." That was the day I stopped talking to him. Though I saw him many times after, I never spoke another word to him as I watched sports on the television in his room.

His sister showed up with a vase of red roses, obviously purchased from the local grocery store. They were placed on the window sill in the chapel just before the service. There were noticeably more people in attendance at this funeral. Jim's sister drove all the way from Wisconsin while members from his Masonic Lodge held a service and as did the men and women of his VFW Post.

The regular pastor entered the room. "Thank God." I said to myself. I didn't hear much of the service as I selfishly reflected on what our lives would be like without Melissa's parents. After the service was over, his sister went over to the window sill and took the flowers back saying, "They would just rot in the cemetery" and I thought, "What an appropriate sendoff."

We drove home in Melissa's father's car, a dark green Lincoln. When they moved into the nursing home, Melissa's parents refused to sell us the car and opted to let it sit idle in the nursing home parking lot. They insisted that I start the car once a week so the engine would not freeze. The irony did not escape me that anything or anyone unattended or unloved will wither up and die. Of course I refused, and eventually they relented and turned the car over to us. It wasn't long before one of our cats climbed in car through an open window, and, sure enough, the next time I got in to drive it, I was greeted by the all too familiar smell of ammonia. Chalk up another karmic deposit.

"I want to get rid of this car," said Melissa. "I get the creeps just being in it."

"It's not that old."

"I know but something about it never felt right to me."

Just before bed, we noticed the cats were unsettled. Lucky sat rigid and alert, his eyes black, as Peter jumped off our bed and ran downstairs. I knew our alarm system was armed and just reckoned it was post-funeral jitters. The next morning I went to get the paper and as I passed the Lincoln, I saw the front windshield of the car had been smashed with no likely culprit (tree limb or rock) in sight.

"Melissa, come see this."

She came to the door. "I told you I wanted to get rid of it. He did this."

My gut tightened and I was glad I had not yet eaten breakfast. Could he have used his last morsel of earthly energy to do this? Maybe this was his demented way of saying "goodbye" or perhaps, "I'm not done torturing you yet."

Shortly after Jim's death, the IRS audited his estate because it was unheard of for any family to pay over half a million dollars to a nursing home. They wanted to make sure there was no more money floating around. Melissa's parents made absolutely sure we would not receive anything in retaliation for us not allowing them to move in just one year after our son was diagnosed with autism. Being an accountant, it was very difficult for me to watch their money go down the drain; however, no amount of money was worth sacrificing our son's wellbeing. Any inheritance would have been impossibly tainted and come at too high a price. Melissa and I made the right decision long ago and had no regrets. Until the day each parent died, Melissa hoped for some sort of resolution with her parents but none ever materialized. And we've never been to their graves. Melissa gave them all she could when they were alive; that was enough.

CHAPTER 40
ONE...

My parents, both in their 80's and in failing health, lived in an elder care facility. They were not saints but, unlike Melissa's parents, had the foresight and grace to make plans to take care of themselves in their senior years.

Early one morning the phone range; it was an aunt calling to say my father had suffered a stroke. "Your mother is at her wit's end," said my aunt. "He won't go to the hospital. Is there anything you can think of to help us get him to go? You know how your father can get."

Six hours until later, Mom, tired and distraught, finally got Dad into a neighbor's car. Relieved to hear that my father had, at last, been reasonable I was stunned to receive another call from my aunt.

"Dean, on the way your mother felt terrible chest pains. As soon as we pulled up to the emergency, they took one look at her and quickly pushed your father to a corner and checked your mother in immediately. She is in cardiology this very minute. I think you should get here. It looks serious for both of them."

I drove down by myself, leaving Melissa and Craig at home. It was a very odd feeling having both parents in the hospital on different floors. They had been members of a huge church for over fifty years, and it seemed like thousands of church members and friends came to visit and wish them well. My parents were loved by so many, yet as their son, I could never reconcile the fact that they did not like me. I remember sitting in the Intensive Care waiting room as the head nurse looked one of the church ministers square in the eyes and said, "Look, I don't care who you are, she needs rest and I am telling you to leave right now."

Thankfully, both my parents survived that hospitalization and we saw them at Easter, but late one summer night the phone rang; it was Robert.

"Hold on while I patch Mom through," said Robert. Then I heard my mother's voice, weak, soft and trembling.

"Your father just had a heart attack," said Mom, sobbing, "and I don't think he is going to make it; the nurses are with him now."

She went on but time for me had stopped. A darkness had enveloped me and I felt nothing. My father died that night and I told Melissa I didn't want Craig at this funeral, either. I begged her to stay home to take care of Craig and the fur balls. It was not easy to convince her, but I finally did. As I left New Jersey and crossed over into Delaware, I remembered all the trips we made back and forth over the years. I saw the year-round Christmas shop on Route 13 and thought how Melissa loved to stop to buy red and gold oversized ribbon, a unique ornament, or hand blown glass. As I passed the 'Welcome to Maryland' sign, I recalled the times we had brought Craig down for sessions in Bethesda with Dr. Stanley Greenspan.

Crossing into Virginia, I drove past my grandparents' old potato farm on the Eastern Shore. Before the Chesapeake Bay Bridge-Tunnel opened, my family had to take the ferry across the Chesapeake Bay, the same one in my recurring dream with my grandmother. As a child, I was always so happy there that I wondered if this place was a part of Heaven.

I was sad to see that my grandparents' farmhouse, where so many happy family gatherings had taken place, was now a crumbling ruin and the 40 acres of rich land they had so painstakingly tended was now overgrown with errant seedlings and weeds. I remembered lying in those fields, star gazing with my cousins. The air was still warm on those the pitch black nights when I saw thousands of specks of light still travelling from the stars, some long dead, and marveled at how their beauty continued to shine for those who took the time to look up in awe and reverence. Then, we would run into the house to hear tales of ghosts and bears as each uncle tried to outdo the other with another outlandish, grisly tale. I suddenly remembered a family birthday party on the Peninsula, where an aunt played an old reel-to-reel tape recording, and, once again, I heard my grandmother's sweet voice. As I drove away, tears streamed down my cheeks.

In just one more month, my parents would have been married sixty-five years. Robert and I had talked about giving them a party but that wouldn't happen now. Many things passed through my mind as I was driving and yes, like Melissa, I thought about our cats. My mind wanted to go anywhere but think about the upcoming funeral. My father, stricken with Stage Three Alzheimer's, had made feeble attempts to apologize to me during our last visit to Hampton. Alzheimer's enabled my father to retrace his steps back through time and contemplate his actions, and he did not like everything he remembered. During my last visit, Dad spoke of things that happened thirty years past thinking it had only been two weeks. I accepted his apologies but words are cheap. Years ago it would have taken so very little to rectify our dysfunctional bond but he chose not to. Melissa thought I was being too harsh and reminded me that her father's last words to her were "Get out, I want to watch the golf game." I was grateful for my father's apology but years ago I had learned more than once not to trust him.

I could not shake the memory of all the times Dad deliberately humiliated me. Each time he did this, it pushed me further and further away until I reached a decision: I vowed that no matter what, I had no intention of being at his side while he was dying. This was not to punish my father but to protect myself from whatever he was going to say to me as he departed. I knew it would be indelible, so for self-preservation, I elected to stay away from his deathbed. Dad had tried, in vain, to convince me that he loved me but his words didn't work when my gut was screaming from my very core.

After a weary, soul searching trip, I arrived in Hampton. The next day I helped Mom and Robert make arrangements for the two hundred people coming to the funeral. The funeral home was bright and airy, almost cheerful; after all, the departed were going *home*. Our family had used it for years and I was familiar with everything, including the cemetery. I stole away to visit my grandmother's grave beside a large oak tree, not far from where Dad was going to be laid to rest. I brushed away leaves from her headstone and wondered if she would be proud of the man who knelt before her.

Robert and I each gave eulogies as Mom sat steely jawed next to Robert's wife. Like Melissa, my mother preferred to shed her tears in private. Robert spoke about how much our father meant to him and how as a very young boy in was in awe of this very large man who came home to him after a hard day at work and played catch. I talked about my father's humor, which was legendary, and how he brought such joy to his friends. He would always make people laugh by saying inane things such as, "I was *so* ugly as a baby, my mother put a pork chop around my neck just so the dog would play with me." He would also say, "The hungriest I ever felt in my life was one hour after a Thanksgiving meal when I decided to go on a diet." They were lame, well-worn jokes, but I could hear laughter in the crowd.

Many of Dad's friends came up to me after the service and congratulated me. They said that I had made them laugh and Dad would have wanted it that way. I asked my mother what she thought of the eulogies and she said, "I could hear your brother's but I couldn't hear a word you said." I should have known better than to even ask. I would always be invisible to her. It amazed me that I still sought her approval, knowing full well that withholding it was my mother's one and only power over me. Still, I was stunned that even at my father's funeral, she couldn't throw me a bone.

Robert and I escorted our mother out of the funeral home to the cemetery where Dad would be laid to rest. On this sweltering July afternoon, all the funeral flowers had wilted as guests gathered around the grave. My mother stood in front of his casket weeping, her eyes glazed and framed with dark circles. The man she spent her life with was gone, and she did not feel whole without him. Then a breeze stirred and leaves on the trees rustled. Once again, a light filled my head. Emotion twisted inside as I sensed my father saying "Thank you, and I love you." As quickly as the light breached my consciousness, it disappeared. Looking at my distraught mother, I suggested that we help her in the car and get her home. Apparently, in death, Dad had heard the eulogy that my Mother could not hear in life.

Two days later, I was back in New Jersey with Melissa and Craig. Melissa was asleep next to me and a cat jumped on the bed. I looked and saw nothing but smiled, I realized Binky's or Onion's spirit had come to comfort me. At this point, only one parent remained and Mom's value was immeasurable to Craig since she was the only family he had left other than us. Craig didn't remember Melissa's parents but she always took the high road whenever we talked about them. This was not to obscure the truth; rather, we believed that whatever happened in the past was not Craig's burden to bear. It was ironic that our cats had more meaning and had given more love to Craig than all four grandparents combined.

CHAPTER 41
PHOENIX RISING

Conspicuous in my natal astrology chart sits a Scorpio Moon, and most astrologers shudder at Scorpio Moons. Scorpio embodies regeneration, and the phoenix is the symbol for the advanced part of Scorpio because it rises from the ashes. Craig was also born with a Scorpio Moon, and he became the *phoenix*.

As Craig grew, magical things began to happen. Like a diamond formed under tremendous pressure, his strength seemed to crystallize and shine brighter in the wake of each storm. As Craig overcame each of his hurdles, I was the proudest father on earth. All the trauma of our lives started to make sense, and the events of our lives no longer seemed random but, somehow, doled out in the correct order. All the times Melissa and I had been burned and found ourselves in the rubble and ashes, we had gotten back up. Our wings may have been a bit tattered and worn but they were spread and soaring. It would prove to be good training for what was to come.

At sixteen, Craig was happy and flourishing. He experienced life in his own way but not so different from everyone else. He attended a private high school for students on the autism spectrum that, on the surface, seemed no different from a typical high school. My son had friends and I saw a very happy young man having a life, as close to normal as possible, surrounded by loving people. How could anyone ask for more than a feeling of belonging within your own personal universe shared by souls with similar interests? What mattered was that he found his niche.

Last year at the school's award dinner, we all entered the catering hall when Craig saw one of his friends and happily walked over to say hello. Melissa and I marveled at the linen table cloths, china, dance floor, and chandeliers. This wonderful school made sure their students had the same experiences as those enjoyed by their counterparts in public schools. In between conversations with the other parents at our table, I nudged Melissa as Craig shyly approached a girl to ask her to dance. He danced with an erratic rhythm but a quick glance at the girl's face told me that she didn't notice. They both looked happy and in their own world.

"I can't believe how far he has come," whispered Melissa, brushing away a tear and knowing that this was just a taste of what life would become. One day, a new bride would nudge Melissa aside and she would no longer be the only woman in her beloved son's life.

"It's because of you."

"No, absolutely not. I may have done the research and played chauffeur, and you worked hard to pay the bills, but Craig did the work. All those years of therapy, three, four times a week. All the doctors we saw and the medications he swallowed that didn't work. He never stopped trusting us and he never gave up the fight."

"Look at him over there dancing. And look, his friends are coming up to him. My God, how I have waited to see this. Do you realize we have grown as people too? Do you think we thought we were blessed fourteen years ago or whenever he was actually diagnosed? I know that I have changed to the very core of my soul. As an accountant, I used to count every penny, and now, I don't care. I will do anything for him and you."

Gazing around the room, I knew Melissa and I weren't alone in our thoughts. Most, if not all, of these families had walked through fire to arrive at this place, and we hadn't journeyed alone. Behind us stood long lines of doctors, school administrators, psychologists, therapists, and, most importantly, the teachers and aides who nurtured, disciplined, and educated our children against what seemed, at times, to be impossible odds. Was it always easy or without conflict? Of course not, but we, as a community, never gave up. We might have been stretched to the breaking point, needed long vacations that we couldn't afford, or a stiff drink at the end of the day, but we never lost faith in the children we held in our care. We honored them too much to let them down.

I loved Craig with all my heart. I am not sure this would have been possible without Melissa and our cats. Every time Craig faced a new developmental hurdle, a new cat would come along beginning with our dear Dash. When he slipped away into the cosmos, another feline rose up in his place to continue his purpose. The irony of life, death, and continuity had been right in front of me all along. My soul had grown, if not our bank account. Almost all of our resources were dedicated to Craig's care which in the beginning, left me drained and demoralized. But now, after spending thousands of dollars over years on outrageous parties for these children and their families, Melissa and I were happy that we were able to give these kids something we never had. We made a difference not only in Craig's life but in the lives of parents like us and their children.

Craig has never said, "I love you, Dad" and, considering my early life, this still pushes buttons deep inside me that continue to fester and ooze. I survived an emotionally fraught childhood, got my act together, and found love with a wonderful woman. Since Craig's birth, I have stood before him ready to make it right and give him all the love I never had, yet he has no need for me to make it right. He can't comprehend the love I'm dying to give but it never was about me, was it? That was my fantasy, not his needs. On some level, I know Craig has always loved me; he just doesn't have the tools to express it. His inability to look me in the eyes and share his soul were part of my blueprint, the one being tread on by furry paws who clearly expressed their feelings but not with words. *Like Craig.* That has always been love in its purest form. So, I had found my purpose through heartache and cats. How many people can say that?

And then it was Melissa's turn.

"Everything keeps falling down," she yelled from the shower. "I dropped a bottle of tomato juice in the market today and then I forgot what I needed. So, it's sandwiches for dinner."

"Ouch," she yelled as I heard a big bar of soap hit her toe like an anvil.

"You okay?" I yelled, but she didn't hear me over the multiple four-letter words spraying from the shower. I opened the shower door and peeked in.

"Honey, would you like me to hold the soap for you?"

No response; she wasn't taking the bait so I tried another tactic.

"Hey, Missy, I have a new name for menopause; how about 'Gravity Challenged?' What do you think?"

Melissa pitched the bar of soap at my head, and I remembered the Manolo Blanik shoe of long ago.

For the next six months, Melissa dropped everything she picked up, cried at the drop of a hat because she could no longer have a baby, was hot, then cold, broke glass after glass in the kitchen and said everything was my fault. I recalled Mrs. Meyers, my piano teacher, nearly burning down her dining room table because she forgot to blow out a candle; she blamed it on "the change." Thank God, we both lived to tell the tale, and once again, a phoenix rises.

CHAPTER 42
TRIUMPH

A compass always points north, though there are four directions. There are also four fundamental feelings from which all others span: pleasure, pain, fear, and sadness, and only one of the four feelings is fun. I learned that you needed to experience all four feelings in order to derive and understand the true value of pleasure. It was necessary for me to find my due north through exploration of the south, east, and west; which path to take is a unique decision. Now, I know my only choice was to take the path that led me to face my problems head on. That path was not easy, but no matter what I endured, I knew when finished, I would have attained true happiness *and* pleasure. There was no other way, no matter what I have been told to believe over the years. An astrologer explained to me that I would always choose the hardest path, but, in my opinion, it has always led me to my bliss. Only a handful of people have actually seen the top of Mount Everest which makes the view all the more magnificent for the chosen few.

One morning I was getting into my car to go to work, when I saw my neighbor on her doorstep bundled in her bathrobe, rubbing hands together to keep them warm. I heard her calling a name but the wind was so fierce I ran over to her to see what was wrong.

"Captain Morgan hasn't come home for days. I've left food out but it hasn't been touched. I'm so worried."

"I'm so sorry," I said, "We'll keep an eye out for him."

As I climbed in my car, I remembered that when animals sensed they were at the end of their lives, they went away to die in solitude which was hard for me to understand. I wondered how an animal that lived with a family for over 15 years could simply walk away. Didn't they want to say goodbye? To be held and stroked in their last hours? Maybe because cats were comfortable in their aloneness, they preferred no distractions, no hindrances, as they made their passage from this life to the next; they left without the burden of unfinished business. It made me wonder if I'd want my loved ones around.

Would I think I had a responsibility to comfort them, instead of wanting them comforting me? Or, would I prefer to be alone, free to focus solely on my journey as the veil between earth and heaven finally parted before me?

Faced with so much death over the past few years, I was looking at my compass for some direction. As three out of four parents had passed, Melissa and I were left with a bag of mixed emotions. During their lives, they had denied us all but the meanest amount of affection, let alone unconditional love. I would never have childhood memories of my father watching me play sports or playing catch with him in the back yard. I understood what a blessing it was to mourn someone with a full and open heart. I mourned grandmother, Ruth and Theo that way, and our cats.

Sometimes I wondered, when I died, would I want to see my parents on the other side? In my dream, my grandmother was the one who welcomed me to the other side but what about Mom and Dad? My gut response was "no" but Melissa would say I was being too harsh again. I know I'd much rather see Theo or Ruth, nimbly sidestepping all the people who hurt me in the past. Maybe my parents wouldn't want to see me? After all, cats forgive; either that or they have very short memories.

It hit me hard when Captain Morgan had walked away. I will always remember him, whiskers splayed and tail high, strutting by our front door holding not one, but two chipmunks, in his mouth. Indeed, Captain Morgan was *King Cat* with the biggest furry ones of all. He was also a bruiser with a tender heart. We nicknamed him "Warrior" and that is exactly what he was till the end. Captain Morgan left with no burdens, no assets - just fond memories. He departed this life with dignity and on his terms. Somehow I understood that Captain knew that. Captain Morgan had chosen his own path to depart *Earth School,* and, after all, that would be a pure definition of triumph.

CHAPTER 43
CONTACTED

So many things happened in my life where I should have seen the hand of God, the other side, or my guardian angel. Instead, I ignored the signs and moved on as if these coincidences were common, everyday occurrences. As I looked back, I understood that I was being molded, guided, and sometimes warned. Any one instance alone might not have much meaning or power but, collectively, as my former landlady Ruth would say, "The man in charge is leaving me alone because he sees that something is happening on the canvas."

Surviving and growing from painful experiences had shaped me into a unique soul, one whose strength was flexible but whose backbone was like rock. Theo once told me my traits were rare; others, under the same pressure, would have collapsed and not been able to fight to survive. Like common elements transformed under tremendous pressure, some people grow strong, their unique facets shining brilliant, like coal to a diamond.

The *veil* appeared to be the essence that kept me from God. When it would occasionally drop around me, tempting me to see through it, I remained stuck on Earth, blocked by my consciousness. Since, I had no recollection of the time before birth, it seemed unlikely that death would be any different. Yet, I struggled every day to understand the meaning of what happens in between and would my soul remember? Or would I crash through the *veil* when my time came, happy and laughing to be back beyond it, away from the fears and heartache of living on Earth? I was left with the knowledge that consciousness had no beginning or end, just like us.

Cats seemed to understand our connection to the Universe. They appeared to know coincidences are not always random events. They know where they belong and their role in the puzzle of my life. Each one has appeared at just the right time to guide me. When Lucky dropped from the sky and into my life, I saw the bluish grey beyond the *veil*, the magic that was just beyond my vision once born. In those moments of epiphany or intense joy, even for a second, I was connected, and my life came together. Karma and destiny were at play.

I listened to the masters in the Universe, philosophers, psychics, who told me the secrets to life, and this is what I gleaned:

> *Enjoy the world and what it has to offer while at the same time tend to your responsibilities. You cannot just work or just play.*

> *You must find balance.*

> *Live in the moment and you will find enlightenment.*

> *You don't have to own anything because it already belongs to you. While sitting on a park bench, it is yours. Otherwise, you have no need for it.*

Cats live like this.

It was one thing to hear someone tell you how to live but quite another to live life, day by day, and figure it out as you go along. On one of my more exotic trips, my boss hired a small boat to take seven of us to a rustic hotel in the middle of the Amazon River. It took three hours to get there, and halfway there, we hit a sand bar. Natives of Peru watched from behind trees, laughing at us, I imagined, because none of us would get out of the boat to push it off the sandbar. At the end of his patience, the driver pointed to me and ordered me down into the murky water. When I looked over the side, I saw the deep water of the well near my grandmother's house. The contrast between the bright sunshine above and the mysteries below sent shivers down my spine - that and the man-eating piranhas swimming just below the surface. Wanting to keep my feet connected to my body, there was no way in hell I was going in.

"No," I said, looking him right in the eye, man to man, my voice deep and strong. Through his glaring eyes, I saw Dad reaching up to me in the barn. With a loud grumble, the driver jumped down and freed the boat from the river bottom. Once again we were on our way, and for the next hour, my boss fretted non stop. All he could say was "I hope this place isn't touristy", and more than one person on the boat wanted to toss him over board. We finally reached our destination, and I gazed at the most beautiful thatched roof hotel, nestled behind leaves the size of elephants, with the sun shining in just the right places. There was no dock so the guide pulled the boat as far up on the muddy bank as he could and then commanded us to get out. This time I complied with suitcase in my hand. I stepped out of the boat and my foot sank ankle deep in the mud. I laughed and looked at my boss saying, "You got your wish, this isn't touristy." Then I felt the tepid water ooze through my sneaker and socks touching my skin, and I immediately remembered the dream with my feet in the mud as I reached desperately for my grandmother.

Later that night, at this amazing hotel in the middle of nowhere, on a bed surrounded by mosquito netting that hung like a veil, the nocturnal animals began to sing their songs. Jungle cats growled, night birds hooted, and a multitude of insects buzzed. With the forest alive and so close, my mind couldn't rest. I stared into the white haze of the netting and let go, yielding to the strength of the "no" I stated on the boat confirming who I was becoming who I am. With eyes open all night, I joined the night sounds and blended with the stars and became the universe, my universe, comfortable in my skin. Sure of my ability, fed by the sights, sounds, and touch of the raw earth, like Binky balancing on the windowsill, I found my footing. I knew my feet, happily still at the bottom of my legs, would carry me through the jungle, the tightly woven greenery wet with life. Without sleep, I rested while I simultaneously received nourishment from nature. Through the netting, in an almost transcendental state, I connected.

Perhaps the astrologer I met so long ago was right about the end of my life. Good things would find me but it seemed a double-edged sword, happy at the end meaning "at the end." I began to feel this was a signal. Theo and I had only seen each other four times, yet his influence on my life was monumental. I thought it was the same as the *veil,* deja vu or whatever you want to call it. Only a small number of connections are necessary to get the job done of bringing you to the correct path in *Earth School.* Melissa and I had many experiences of light bulb moments, when the truth was revealed. It was like seeing a cat with feathers in its mouth. There was no mistaking what was going on - no doubt. You knew what was real, yet all you saw were the feathers. The chunk of life gobbled down had to digest before we could gain any sustenance from it.

CHAPTER 44
MIDDLE CLAW

How could I live this life in any other way but like a cat? The cats became the mirror of my soul, assisting me through a cathartic and positive metamorphosis that will stay with me always. Perhaps this is why cats can't look in a mirror. They are mirrors themselves.

Call me crazy. I believe it was my destiny to live my adult life with Melissa, Craig, and the cats. Cats came into my life in the same way I found Melissa and Theo, by chance or by fate. They recognized my moods and helped me just by being there with their love that knew no limits. However, life with the kitties was not always roses: hairballs in shoes, sinks used as litter pans, a dead vole brought to my pillow, birds carted into the house to be shredded beyond recognition, and tens of thousands of dollars of vet bills. It was always easy to forgive the cats for their transgressions because they were innocent. Forgiving people was not as easy.

Over the span of my life, I had crystallized a lot of pent up anger and carried it on my back like Atlas carried the world. Maybe that's why I was so insistent on calling d'Artagnan the "Onion." I was the onion created layer upon layer to protect my core from the world. I had spent countless years avoiding pain when the secret was there all along: forgiveness and not repeating past behavior. To be sure, this was always easier said than done. All that pent up energy could have been constructively directed to win a Nobel Prize but, instead, I chose to keep the anger alive to fester and rot away my soul. I needed to emotionally connect to whatever happened years ago, confront the pain, and move on. After all, if a meteorite falls to the earth and damages my car, does it make sense for me to spend the rest of my life being angry at a rock?

Now, after directly confronting that pain, it is gone and I wonder why I spent so much energy avoiding the knowledge or feeling the pain. The layers of the onion I built over a lifetime were stripped one by one, cat by cat, on constant duty to patiently navigate me through this mystery of life. Over the years, their middle claws have plucked away at the *veil*, now frayed with only a few thin threads still remaining. With their assistance, my soul is now prepared for what's to come, the avatars of my salvation have shown me the way.

The past three years have flown by. Craig's in college and is now living with his girlfriend. I'm not supposed to tell his mother, but in her newfound career as a real estate agent, she found out anyway. Ironically, I met his girlfriend the same day my doctor told me I had heart disease. I was proud and happy for Craig but worried about my future. She is very cute with dark brown hair and brown eyes, and I am worried that I won't live to see my grandchildren. I have so much to tell them.

A sudden flash of light awakens me to the searing pain tearing at my body. As consciousness grips me, I see Melissa, but this time it's for real and her beautiful, green eyes fill with tears as she looks at me. I squeeze her hand. Lying here, I realize my life has just flashed before me: so many heartaches, so much love between us. I look again in her eyes and she nods as if she is saying "It's okay to go." I have seen her face looking just like this so many times before as she has said good bye to her beloved cats.

A sudden thump at my feet draws my attention and I look to see if one of the cats jumped on our bed but the sheets are white, Melissa hates white sheets. I'm not at home. I'm in a hospital or perhaps I am on a vet table like so many of Melissa's cats before me, but I see Onion sitting crouched at my feet, a soft radiance surrounding him. He's looking at me with such kindness. What's happening? I turn to Melissa and try to tell her that I love her but the words don't come. So, with my eyes, without words, I tell her, like Onion told me. I have travelled through the years of my life so fast. I feel my life is coming to its end.

An uncomfortable pressure grows in my chest, like a fist pressing down, without mercy, on my heart. Another shadow gently ambles to me on four soft paws. It effortlessly navigates its way over a myriad of wires and tubes before coming to rest on my pillow, lying wreathed around my head like an invisible diadem of infinite grace. It's too bright in here. I open my mouth to complain but I can't breathe. A machine screeches and I hear Melissa say something. It doesn't hurt anymore.

I look down at my body as I float away and Melissa appears smaller. I yearn to say "I love you" one more time but the words don't materialize. I search for Craig and see him at his apartment with his girlfriend. I remain earth-bound long enough to listen to the words I've waited a lifetime to hear, "I miss Daddy and I love him." With that simple sentence, Craig saved my life. His words gave meaning to everything I lived for, all the soul searching necessary for me to help him without concern for myself, money or anything else. I'm enveloped in their love; the love our family experienced with me, Melissa, Craig, and the cats. It was real and I already miss them.

My attention now turns to what is before me; it is the *veil*. I breach its borders, a few strands of brilliant colored thread, drift in my wake. I am back at the familiar creek just at the edge of the Chesapeake Bay where I spent many happy summer days clamming and crabbing with my Grandma. The water stills smells brackish but my feet are no longer small. Sure of my purpose, I happily splash the water in sparkling arcs that turn to rainbows in the bright noonday sun. Against a robin's egg sky, I see the old ferry terminal and hear a deep bass horn. The white ship heads straight for me cutting effortlessly through dead calm water. I am ready. I see my grandmother holding the rail. She is young and dressed in her Sunday best. As the boat comes to a gentle cessation, I stretch out by hand to her, and this time I hold on. She pulls me up and into her arms. With such pride, she motions her hand for me to behold what I have been yearning to see my entire life. I see the brightest blue white light everywhere, and my soul becomes soaked with love as the plasma conducts the flow. All the disconnected pieces of my life suddenly come together like a jigsaw puzzle but I see in her eyes, a wistful sorrow, "Dean, you can't stay. I was sent to tell you that you must return; your family needs you. Craig will need you to show him how to be a good father. I will be here when it is truly your time. I love you so much."

Just as I try to tell her that I love her, the intense pain returns. I see her mischievous smile, and the last thing I hear is my grandmother calling, "…. and, Dean, cut back on the beef and bourbon."

I don't know how long I have been away. A breathing tube irritates my throat, and the IV's in my arms are uncomfortable. I barely see Melissa but I feel her hand where my grandmother's was just seconds ago. She says I have had surgery and everything will be okay. I know my purpose now as I look into her soul, through those lovely green eyes, where I also see Craig's. My God, it all makes perfect sense.

EPILOGUE

A few weeks later, I am recovering in my bed upstairs, trying not to cough or laugh. I hear the bang of the front door as Melissa and Craig, who has temporarily moved back home to help out, return with groceries. Craig runs up the stairs with the biggest grin on his face and I knew something was going on.

"Okay," I said. "Tell me what's up?"

Craig tries to answer but he is unable to hold back his laughter. Melissa appears at our bedroom door with that all too familiar guilty look.

"Dad, on the way to grocery store I saw a sign at the animal shelter that said 'Tabby Tuesdays.' I told Mom and sure enough they were having a sale on tabby kittens so she pulled into the parking lot."

"How many cats did you get," I sighed in disgust. "I have made it very clear to your Mother that our limit is four."

"Dad, we didn't get any cats," said Craig.

"Why not?" I said, puzzled.

"Mom bought you a puppy!"